With satisfaction, Nikolai saw that Ellie did indeed remember what had happened between them that night

The longing and desire that had been inexorably building in his blood ever since she had opened the door and allowed him into her room increased with the most stunning force.

Exhaling softly, he moved the pad of his thumb from her bewitchingly full lower lip to trace her fine-boned jawline until finally he cupped it in his hand. Pleasure and need drowned him. The extremely erotic scent she exuded and the warmth from her soft, sweetly curvaceous body had him all but hypnotized. And it only added to the agony of pleasure inside him when he hazarded a guess that underneath her insubstantial robe, she was naked.

For a long moment Nikolai's body and mind were locked in a battle for supremacy over his desire. Primal instinct vied with a logic he really did not want to entertain—and logic was losing fast. The living, breathing reality of this woman was simply too much temptation for one mortal man.

Dear Reader,

Harlequin Presents® is all about passion, power and seduction, along with oodles of wealth and abundant glamour. This is the series of the rich and the superrich. Private jets, luxury cars and international settings that range from the wildly exotic to the bright lights of the big city! We want to whisk you away to the far corners of the globe and allow you to escape to and indulge in a unique world of unforgettable men and passionate romances. There is only one Harlequin Presents®. And we promise you the world....

As if this weren't enough, there's more! More of what you love every month. Two weeks after the Presents® titles hit the shelves, four Presents® EXTRA titles go on sale! Presents® EXTRA is selected especially for you—your favorite authors and much-loved themes have been handpicked to create exclusive collections for your reading pleasure. Now there are more excuses to indulge! Each month, there's a new collection to treasure—you won't want to miss out.

Harlequin Presents®—still the original and the best!

Best wishes,

The Editors

Maggie Cox

BOUGHT: FOR HIS CONVENIENCE OR PLEASURE?

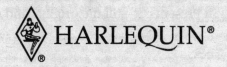

HARLEQUIN®

TORONTO • NEW YORK • LONDON
AMSTERDAM • PARIS • SYDNEY • HAMBURG
STOCKHOLM • ATHENS • TOKYO • MILAN • MADRID
PRAGUE • WARSAW • BUDAPEST • AUCKLAND

ISBN-13: 978-0-373-12847-1

BOUGHT: FOR HIS CONVENIENCE OR PLEASURE?

First North American Publication 2009.

All about the author...
Maggie Cox

MAGGIE COX loved to write almost as soon as she learned to read. Her favorite occupation was daydreaming and making up stories in her head; this particular pastime has stayed with her through all the years of growing up, starting work, marrying and raising a family. No matter what was going on in her life, whether happiness, struggle or disappointment, she'd go to bed each night and lose herself in her imagination.

Through all the years of her secretarial career she filled exercise books and later her word processor with her writing, never showing anyone what she wrote and basically keeping her stories for her own enjoyment. It wasn't until she met her second husband and the love of her life that she was persuaded to start sharing those stories with a publisher. Maggie settled on Harlequin, as she had loved romance novels since she was a teenager and read at least one or two paperbacks a week. After several rejections, the letters sent back from the publisher started to become more and more positive and encouraging. In July 2002 she sold her first book, *A Passionate Protector,* to the Harlequin Romance® line.

The fact that she is being published is truly a dream come true. However, each book she writes is still a journey in "courage and hope" and a quest to learn and grow and be the best writer she can. Her advice to aspiring authors is: "Don't give up at the first hurdle, or even the second, third or fourth, but keep on keeping on until your dream is realized. Because if you are truly passionate about writing and learning the craft, as Paulo Coelho states in his book *The Alchemist,* 'The universe will conspire to help you' make it a reality."

To Conar and Sandy

You mean the world to me, my beautiful boys!

CHAPTER ONE

'Do YOU remember what happened, Elizabeth?'

His voice sounded as if it came from a long distance away—like a voice in a dream. Drifting in and out of consciousness, Ellie didn't try particularly hard to stay focused. Somehow the sensation of cotton wool nothingness that had been cocooning her seemed far more appealing right at that moment than anything else. There was a great desire to sink back into its warmth and protection as quickly as possible, and avoid experiencing the all too unsettling wave of discomfort and fear that kept flowing through her like rivulets of ice every time she became conscious.

Something bad had happened. Why was this man forcing her to try and remember it? For a scant moment her eyes fixed on his hard, chiselled face, but she quickly closed them again because studying the unforgiving rigid lines of jaw, mouth and cheekbone that confronted her made her feel bad somehow…as if she'd done something wrong…something *really* wrong. *If only she could remember what it was.*

Yet maybe it was best that she didn't remember. Thankfully, the cottonwool fuzziness returned just in time. No more trying to recall things that might cause pain and distress. She was in hospital. That much she *did* know. That was quite enough knowledge of her predicament to be going on with…

He cut a sombre, rather intimidating figure in his black suit, and she wondered vaguely if he might be in mourning for someone. Why was he there almost every time she opened her eyes? What was he waiting for?

The tantalising threads of some kind of personal connection hovered frustratingly close, but right then the final link was beyond her. However, the sickening feeling persisted that *she* had been the cause or at least the catalyst for something dreadful. Deliberately veering her thoughts away from trying to imagine what, she focused on the plain, uninspiring room, with its nondescript oatmeal-coloured walls and the hospital scent that permeated everything around her. She sensed a heaviness in the lower part of her body. Glancing down, she realised for the first time that both her legs were in plaster. Making a little sound of distress, she turned her cheek into the pillow and again shut her eyes…

One day not long afterwards Ellie woke up to a face she *did* remember…and it belonged to her father.

'Don't worry, my girl.' He patted her hand as though she were a small, defenceless child. 'Your old man knows what to do. I'm going to take you away from all this just as soon as I can. Tommy Barnes knows a thing or two about how to blend into the background and disappear. I haven't spent the last twenty years doing what I do without learning a few tricks!'

'Make-up's ready for you now, Dr Lyons. Just follow Susie, will you? She'll take care of you.'

Ellie really couldn't attest to enjoying being a guest on these anodyne afternoon television programmes. Neither had she particularly taken to the label the London media had dubbed her with ever since she'd helped the drug-addicted son of a high profile politician who had been living on the streets. 'The pony-tailed psychologist'. It made her feel about fifteen, and Ellie abhorred the idea of ever being that young and inexperienced again. Some things in life *did* get better with age, she'd found. The path that had led her to where she was now had been strewn with quite a few large rocks, but even so she had managed to survive the journey and make a good life for herself.

And the most surprising thing of all was that her dad had helped—in his own muddled, haphazard, seat-of-the-pants way. He'd come up trumps for Ellie after her accident five years ago, and moving from London to Scotland had been one of the best moves of her life. It had definitely given her added impetus to complete her studies in psychology and qualify for the work she'd longed to do.

About a year ago an opportunity had come for her to return to London and work in the East End at a project that was particularly dear to her heart—the plight of young people sleeping rough on the streets. Knowing something about feeling abandoned and alone, she knew a great urge to help as many of these kids as she could. But for this week at least she was located south of the river—staying at a charming little bijou hotel in Chelsea, not far from the Kings Road, funded by the cable TV company that had hired her to do a week-long special on the troubled teenage off-spring of some B-list celebrities.

She could have done without this particular obliga-tion. The small counselling practice she had set up in Hackney was growing, and what with her commitments at the centre for the homeless she needed to be back where she could do the most good—doing the 'real' work she'd studied so hard for. But the money for this particular stint was too good to turn down. The profile she'd unwittingly earned was at least helping Ellie to plough some money back into the centre, and she would continue to do whatever she could to help increase the meagre funding the project struggled to get by on.

Back at the hotel, after Ellie had done the show, she was waylaid by the young receptionist, with her perfect plum-coloured crop and smoothly ironed uniform, as she stepped through the revolving door into the foyer.

'There's someone waiting to see you, Dr Lyons. I've shown him into one of the meeting rooms along the corridor, so that you can have a little privacy. Room number one.'

Immediately wary, Ellie frowned. She couldn't be too careful in her line of work, she'd found. Because of its nature, people sometimes got angry, and occasionally even tried to seek her out to give her a piece of their mind. It was the last thing she felt like doing—placating some irate viewer, or a relative of someone she'd tried to help or advise.

'Who is he?' Ellie enquired. 'Did he leave a name?'

She tried to stifle a yawn as the young receptionist swept her with a curious, interested glance. Unspoken was her realisation that this was someone seriously impressive—and what had he to do with someone like Ellie?

'Mr Nikolai Golitsyn,' she announced, with some authority.

'Are you sure?'

Ellie's legs had turned into a river, sucking all her strength down, deep down, into its surging, heaving depths. Her head started to swim and for a moment her gaze went out of focus. *Nikolai Golitsyn...* It was a name that haunted her dreams and belonged to a man who had caused her more tumult than even her wayward father had done. Although she dreaded seeing him again, underneath that dread was a longing that had not lessened in its emotional intensity over the passage of time.

'I'm perfectly sure, Dr Lyons!' The receptionist took umbrage at the mere suggestion she might have got her facts wrong.

No longer tired, but acutely awake and alert as if she dangled off a cliff edge with bloody fingernails and a thousand feet drop below her onto treacherous sharp rocks, Ellie chewed down anxiously on her lip. *How had he found her after all this time*? Her father had covered their tracks so carefully—even suggesting she take up her mother's maiden name and shorten Elizabeth to

'Ellie'. But her reluctant recent high profile had pre-sented the very real possibility that her previous employer *would* at last discover her whereabouts, and from time to time she had nervously contemplated that.

Touching the tips of her fingers to her neatly tied back wheat-blonde hair, Ellie wasn't surprised to feel them tremble. The sheer dread that surged through her blood made her feel dangerously weak for a second.

'Thank you,' she murmured to the girl behind the desk.

'You're welcome!'

All offence at Ellie's possible doubt in her compe-tence banished—the girl's answering smile was as bright as a May full moon. *It was the smile of someone who'd been raised within the warmth and comfort of loving family, with friends around her to cushion life's blows. Someone who had yet to learn that life could be hard.*

Unable to prevent the wave of envy that washed over her, Ellie patted down some stray fair hairs she'd dis-lodged from her ponytail, then smoothed down the trousers of her smart black trouser-suit. Trying hard not to feel like a condemned prisoner, she headed down the thickly carpeted corridor to the designated meeting room.

'Hello.'

The everyday greeting that she automatically offered sounded incongruous even to Ellie's own hearing.

The man seated at the long, highly polished meeting table—drumming his fingers as though his patience had already been stretched to extreme limits—rose slowly to his feet. At the very first glance he exuded the kind of electricity and energy that made the air feel charged and potent. He was tall and—although lean—clearly packed the kind of toned, ruthlessly honed muscle beneath his clothes that could easily intimidate. In fact that was an understatement. Those broad, iron-hard shoulders nestling beneath the finest bespoke tailoring would surely give an attacking army pause?

The personal emotional threat he represented to Ellie was like a hovering menace that rattled her peace of mind and all that she had worked so hard for, and she sucked in a steadying breath. Seeing his military-cut fair hair and still-chiselled features, her initial assessment of his appearance was that the intervening years had been kind to Nikolai Golitsyn…but the bitterness edging his mouth and the cheekbones that slanted like cruel gashes in his face told a *different* story.

'Elizabeth.'

The ice-blue eyes narrowed searchingly, and Ellie sensed the piercing, laser-like quality of them, feeling a helpless shiver of disquiet and fear down her back.

'I prefer to be called Ellie these days.' She sounded defensive, and more than a little scared, and she couldn't help but despise herself for it. Where was her training when she needed it?

'I am sure you do.' The Russian's lip curled cynically. 'I am sure you would have preferred to remain anonymous for the rest of your life as far as I am concerned—but you should have known that was never going to be remotely possible. And you have helped my case considerably by putting yourself in the public eye. I confess my surprise that you did so, but perhaps you grew too confident that I would have given up my search for you a long time ago? If that it is true then you have only yourself to blame for your arrogance!'

The compelling face before her hardened like a glacier, and Ellie's stomach plunged like a stone. By now she had hoped to be enjoying a long hot bath in her suite, mulling over the day and the two new clients she had acquired for the programme. *Not* coming face to face for the first time in five years with the man who had caused her to flee the city she'd grown up in because he'd blamed her for causing his brother's death!

Her throat felt dry as scorched earth, and Ellie longed for a glass of cool water to ease the discomfort. 'I have nothing to either hide or run away from any more!' she declared. 'The only reason I left like I did was because my father was concerned about me. He wanted to take me to a place where I could properly recover from my injuries and recuperate!'

'I do not believe that was the only reason you disappeared as you did. Otherwise why the change of name— *Dr Lyons*?' Stating her name—her new name—with ironic disdain, Nikolai walked towards her.

Ellie froze, no longer wishing for a cool drink but instead for some benevolent divine force to intercede and suddenly make her invisible. But disappearing was only ever going to be a temporary reprieve. She'd always known that. Much better to stand and confront her demons no matter how intimidating they were!

Garnering all her courage, she schooled herself not to show fear—but it wasn't easy. Even five years ago— his hair fashionably longer, and the skin across his sculpted features more relaxed, less stretched and spare—Nikolai Golitsyn had made her wary. There'd been something about him…something provocative, enigmatic and powerful…that had made her muscles clench with tension whenever she'd found herself in his company. His brother Sasha had once goaded Ellie with his assertion that Nikolai had a ruthless streak that would shock her to her bones, should she ever have cause to anger him, and that forgiveness just wasn't part of his make-up. Once you got on the wrong side of him…look out!

But then Sasha *would* have said that. He had always been jealous of his more successful, enigmatic older brother. His own easy charm had won him many friends, but Nikolai's dependable solidity and hard-working ethic won him the respect and admiration that the younger man had craved. Ellie had learned that from day one in her role as nanny to Sasha and her sister Jackie's baby girl, in the imposing Park Lane house where she had agreed to live after Jackie had died in childbirth.

The brothers' rows had made the walls shake, she remembered. But despite what Sasha had asserted Nikolai had always seemed to be the first to want to heal any rifts.

'Why did you come to see me?' she asked now, willing her pounding heart to somehow calm down as Nikolai drew nearer.

'You can ask me that? After all that has happened?'

He spoke several languages besides his native Russian, and his English was near perfect. But right then his native accent was unmistakable—even pronounced. Beneath it seethed a vast sea of anger and resentment. All directed towards *her*.

'What happened to Sasha was the most t-terrible thing,' Ellie stuttered. 'I'm willing to talk to you—of course I am—but there's nothing new I can tell you about what happened, I'm afraid.'

'Is that so?'

'I know these years since you lost your brother must have been very hard for you, but my hope has always been that when we met again you would somehow have come to realise that the accident wasn't my fault, and that we could move away from any suggestion of blame or recrimination.'

'Is that what you hoped? Well, I have to advise you that such futile hope is both a travesty and a complete waste of time! Instead of talking to me after the inquest, which is what you should have done, or at least seeing for yourself that your niece was all right, you chose to run away with your disreputable father. Since then have clearly made a pleasant and successful life for yourself! Of course you want that to continue! But now you must begin to realise that it might not. Why you agreed to drive Sasha that day in *my* car, when you had only just passed your test and I had told him to stay put until I returned, has dogged my every waking hour. Trust me when I tell you I will not rest until I finally learn the reason!'

Nikolai had barked that question at Ellie outside the court on the day of the inquest, and her father had put his arm round her and sworn at him in his daughter's defence.

'Leave her alone!' he had cried. 'Don't you think she's been through enough?'

Again Ellie longed for a drink to help lubricate her painfully dry throat.

'I still can't tell you the reason. You surely can't have forgotten that I hurt my head in the accident and lost all memory of what happened that day? In all this time I'm sorry to say it's never returned. It's like a lost piece of a jigsaw that I just can't find…no matter how hard I try. The doctors told me at the hospital that it could return all of a sudden or maybe not at all. I'm sorry if you find that hard to accept, but it's the truth!'

'How very convenient for you!'

Experiencing genuine heartfelt anguish at Nikolai's caustic response, Ellie linked her hands tightly together in front of her. Did he think it was easy for her, losing the memory of a whole day? No matter how terrible it had been? Some might say it was a blessing, but all she knew was that doubt, fear and guilt had lain heavy on her heart ever since—because she couldn't even remember *why* she would have got into a car with Sasha and driven when she had barely passed her test.

Although charming, Sasha had been reckless and unpredictable, and losing Jackie had seemed to unbalance him even more. He had made no attempt to bond with his baby daughter at all and, if Nikolai hadn't stepped in and given her a home the child would have been starved of all the love and affection that was her birthright, Ellie was sure. But it was Sasha's seriously addictive behaviour that had disturbed Ellie the most, she remembered.

'It's not convenient for me in any way! How could you say such a thing? Don't you think what happened left its scars on *me*? And I'm not just talking about physical ones!'

'Yes. You would know all about the psychological scars of such a trauma, would you not, Dr Lyons? Especially the ones associated with extreme guilt!'

Ellie actually stepped away from the man confronting her, because his barely contained fury seriously disturbed her. The smartly furnished conference room suddenly felt like a tomb to her, and she grasped at her rapidly melting composure. But the seams holding back strong emotions from the aftermath of that distressing time were slowly bursting apart.

'I don't deny that I have guilt—but that's because I left Arina, not because I know I caused the accident! How can I admit to such a dreadful thing when I don't even remember what happened?' she cried.

'My brother was only twenty-eight years old, Elizabeth… Too young to die so senselessly. Not to know why he died in such a way means that I cannot simply lay his spirit to rest and forget! What do I tell his daughter when she is grown? Have you ever thought about that?'

Feeling numb, Ellie couldn't find the words to answer him.

'The fact that he died is not the worst of it! What I cannot forgive is that when you decided to get into the car with him and take the wheel you also took Arina along for the ride! She was just a baby! What could you have been thinking?'

Ellie knew that Arina had survived the terrible accident that had killed her father and maimed her nanny and aunt without a scratch on her, strapped securely into her baby seat. The collision they'd had mercifully only crushed the front of the car, leaving the back miraculously intact. The Divine had *definitely* been looking out for the infant that dreadful day, and Ellie had often wept with gratitude. She could never have left if she had known the child was hurt. If she had been killed along with her father, Ellie would have wanted to die too! The thought that the little girl might have been harmed in any way still had the power to give her nightmares…

'How can I answer that? Haven't you been listening to anything I've said? I took my responsibilities extremely seriously as far as looking after my niece was concerned, and all I know is I would never have done anything to put her in jeopardy!'

'But you *did* put her in jeopardy—did you not, Elizabeth? She could easily have been killed along with her father!' Nikolai threw her the most contemptuous glance imaginable, and right then Ellie honestly *did* feel like dying.

But she quickly reminded herself she'd suffered enough regret and distress to last her ten lifetimes, and knew it would serve no purpose whatsoever to ceaselessly revisit those debilitating emotions. Life moved on. *She* had moved on—even if the man in front of her hadn't. It still appeared that he wanted to punish and blame her for what had happened to his brother.

Hugging her arms over her chest, Ellie moved her head slowly from side to side. 'I would never have allowed anything or anyone to harm the baby… I adored her! I—I… '

'What?'

'I loved her… I still love her.'

It was obvious that Nikolai was in no mood to listen to reason. But Ellie's compassion as well as her training told her that she needed to remember he was in pain too. He had lost his only brother, and had suffered the shock of learning that his beloved baby niece had been in the car too. She had to forgive him his anger and resentment, even if it wasn't in her power to reveal to him what had really happened that day. But *he* had to accept that five years had gone by. What did he want Ellie to do? Give up on her own future because she had lived and Sasha hadn't? Was that the punishment he wanted to exact? No doubt he was furious about the perceived success she had made of her life since the accident, and the irony of that was hardly lost on her. She didn't *feel* like a success.

'I understand your need to know what happened. I really do.' She shrugged sympathetically, and the most illogical hope suddenly surfaced inside her. Could she somehow make contact with the more human side of him? Was she crazy even to try?

Nikolai Golitsyn had always been an enigma to her: reserved, self-contained and sometimes chillingly aloof. When Ellie had first worked for him she had often wondered what it would take to breach those iceberg-like walls he seemed so frequently to retreat behind when in company. Occasionally she had been party to glimpses of intriguing warmth in his character—especially when he'd been around his small niece—and that had provoked Ellie's helpless interest in the man even more. The idea that there was some softness lurking somewhere inside that intimidating frame of his had been disturbingly appealing.

'Don't you think I'd like to know too? I feel like a sculpture that's accidentally had too much stone chipped away. It's left me feeling hollow and uneven inside. And I know…I know that I'll never be the same again.'

Nikolai slid his hand into his trouser pocket and sighed deeply—but without the smallest trace of sympathy. 'Whether your memory returns or not, you and I have some unfinished business—and there is no escaping that fact!' His jaw visibly hardened. 'You will soon learn that there are consequences for running away like you did, Elizabeth.'

Ellie blanched, 'Consequences?'

'I have to go now. But I have a table booked in the hotel restaurant in a couple of hours' time. I will expect you to join me there for dinner. Do not even think of refusing me!'

There was a knock at the door and, unable to disguise his impatience, Nikolai called out, 'Yes?'

A large man with close-cropped hair, immaculately suited and with the kind of physical frame that suggested moving mountains would be as easy as treading on an ant to him, put his head round the door. Remembering that from time to time Nikolai employed the use of such men as bodyguards, Ellie shivered. The man spoke briefly in Russian, and Nikolai answered equally as briefly. The man left.

'I am late for my next meeting,' Nikolai snapped, as if it were entirely Ellie's fault.

She touched a nervous but indignant hand to a button

on her jacket and frowned. 'You sound like you're looking for some kind of revenge… Is that it?'

Even as she articulated the words her body started to tremble. Chillingly, her reaction only seemed to amuse Nikolai. He smiled, and she watched his broad shoulders lift in a careless shrug.

'Call it what you will, *Dr Lyons*… But however you like to refer to it… however you might psychoanalyse what appears to be a crude desire on my part to make you suffer…just know that you *will* pay!"

CHAPTER TWO

THE *change in her was subtle, but nevertheless arresting.* After his encounter with Elizabeth, Nikolai had for the first time in years sat through a business meeting and not been able to give the matter in hand his full and utmost attention. His usually meticulous and organised mind had been completely hijacked by thoughts about Arina's aunt and former nanny.

Now, as he entered the lift of the same hotel she was staying in, to go up to his suite—he had made the reservation as soon as his sources had informed him that she would be staying there—he reflected on the meeting they had had, his mind and body in turmoil. For so long Elizabeth Barnes's whereabouts had consumed him, and he had begun to believe that disturbing memories of her would be all he'd ever have. Then he had chanced to catch a glimpse of her on television being interviewed—and discovered that she was Dr Ellie Lyons now.

Nikolai had barely been able to think straight, he had been so shocked and furious. But beneath his rage and tumult were feelings that were not so easily explained or quantified. He seemed to be gripped by something unnameable and compelling that existed just below the surface of his everyday thoughts about her.

A wave of memory submerged him. When he had seen her last she had been almost coltishly lean. Now, five years had developed those youthful angles into the most arresting curves. Her face, which had always verged on being breathtaking—with those luminously clear rain-washed eyes and that soft curving mouth—had become even more so. And the lustrous corn-coloured hair tied back in that businesslike ponytail was the perfect setting to showcase such beauty. *She was an absolute gift to the world of television.* Not only was she a practising psychologist at a time when the world seemed fascinated by other people's relationship problems and wanted to hear them discussed on a regular basis, but she looked like a flaxen-haired angel too!

Torn and angered by the troubling direction of his thoughts, Nikolai flexed his fingers and willed the lift to reach his floor. The last thing he wanted to do was admit that Elizabeth's beauty disturbed him! There was far too much at stake here for him to become sidetracked or distracted by her undoubted physical appeal… especially when the lady had categorically proved she absolutely could not be trusted.

Once inside the plush hotel suite, his body brimming with the kind of restless energy that could not be contained, Nikolai opted to go back downstairs to the gym. Starting to disrobe on his way to the bedroom, he discarded his jacket and tie and then started on the buttons of his Savile Row shirt. Lifting some weights and running on the treadmill would help pass the time until dinner, when he and his reluctant companion would meet up once again.

He grimaced bitterly at the thought, at that moment feeling nothing but resentment and a desire to punish where she was concerned. Kicking off his handmade leather shoes, he arrived in the bedroom, but barely registered its fine furnishings and understated elegance. Having inherited an oil business from his father at just twenty-four, to him hotel rooms—however opulent and well appointed—were merely a necessary convenience, that was all. He much preferred to return home after meetings whenever possible, and as he owned several houses all over the world home could be any place he chose.

When he was in London, he and Arina resided at the house in Park Lane from where, on that fateful day five years ago, Elizabeth had driven his brother Sasha to some unknown destination…

For months after her aunt's disappearance Arina had sobbed herself to sleep most nights, unable to be soothed by either Nikolai or the first of what had turned out to be a stream of hopeful replacement nannies. None of them had forged the almost maternal bond Elizabeth had. How could they? Undoubtedly the blood-ties the infant shared with her aunt had helped her form a strong attachment to her, and Arina had clearly been disturbed by the fact she was no longer in her life.

What Nikolai could not forgive was that, knowing such a bond existed between them, Elizabeth had still callously deserted them without so much as a hint that she planned to leave so suddenly. Add to that the shocking discoveries that had been brought to light after the accident—a family heirloom found in the car after it had crashed, clearly stolen, plus his increasing belief that Elizabeth must have been having an affair with Sasha for her to commit such a reckless act as to drive the car for him—Nikolai had barely known how to subdue the rage that had consumed him.

When she had absconded after the inquest he had utilised a lot of time, money and expert help in trying to locate her whereabouts, and her disappearance had caused him no end of sleepless nights and stress-filled days. What had *really* happened on the day of the accident? He *burned* to know. Elizabeth's sudden flight had screamed her guilt to the rooftops, and it had definitely fuelled Nikolai's desire to somehow make her pay. Whatever else transpired, that terrible day had robbed him of his brother and Arina of her father—and she had definitely played her part in the tragedy that had taken place.

Now that she eluded him no longer she would quickly see that the perfect little life she had fashioned for herself for the past five years was definitely going to undergo some radical changes—one way or another…

Ellie chose a simply designed black cocktail dress to wear to dinner. The irony of the colour was not lost on her. Ever since she'd set eyes on Nikolai Golitsyn again it was as though a violent darkening storm had threatened the pleasant meadow she'd been walking in, and truth to tell she was frightened. It hadn't sat well with her all these years that she'd agreed to fall in with her father's advice to simply disappear and then get herself a whole new identity, but at the time she'd been far too traumatised to argue. *Recent events had prompted even more painful reflection.*

Her father had been diagnosed with Parkinson's disease, and although his illness had undoubtedly forged a closer bond between them, and she perfectly understood why he had taken her away, Ellie wished she'd fought her ground and stayed to talk to Nikolai. Maybe if she'd stayed he would have eventually stopped blaming her for Sasha's death, realised that somehow his brother *must* have had a major part in events given his proclivity to be both reckless and intoxicated? In time he might even have come to accept that Ellie really *couldn't* recall what had happened that day and forgiven her at last.

If all that had transpired then she would still be looking after her niece now, and wouldn't be burdened by the most dreadful guilt that she *had* indeed abandoned her sister's child in her hour of need. But, even though she had a deep and abiding regret about leaving so suddenly, Ellie believed her father had acted with the best of intentions too. By being there in *her* hour of need she knew he had somehow hoped to make it up to her for all his years of emotional and physical neglect of her and Jackie when they were younger.

Fear of the consequences if her fate should be left to Nikolai had also inspired his actions. A man who had such enormous wealth and power at his fingertips could never be trusted, her father had warned. It would be like living with a time-bomb! If he chose to bring a private case against Ellie she would have little defence, considering that she had lost her memory. There was no telling how he and his fancy lawyers might twist things to their advantage! Yes…it was better that she had moved right away from him, until the sorrows and mistakes of the past were a little less raw and blunted by the passing of time…

Staring at her reflection now in the full-length mirror, Ellie touched a trembling hand to the balconette bodice of her dress, with its simple shoestring straps. *God! She looked as pale as sugar frosting!* What she wouldn't give for a little sun in some warmer climes, to bronze her skin and brighten her up! But that was going to be impossible, given her schedule at both the practice and the centre. Add to that this recent bout of television work, and she'd be lucky to grab a moment she could call her own…let alone have a holiday!

But her disappointment about not being able to look forward to a break paled into insignificance when Ellie thought about meeting up with Nikolai again. Her stomach lurched. It was unlikely she'd be able to swallow even a morsel of food all evening, confronted with his glowering accusing face across the table! He had looked even more frighteningly fit and intimidating then she'd remembered, and Ellie knew he had meant every word of that threat he'd left her with earlier… There would be were consequences for what he saw as her cold-hearted desertion…

* * *

'I took the liberty of getting us a table where we would have privacy.'

I'll bet you did! Ellie thought nervously as she sat in the padded velvet chair the smartly suited *maître d'* had pulled out for her. Tucked away in the most secluded corner of the hotel's elegant dining room, with its artistic silk panelling on the walls and its brass chandeliers fashioned in intricate Celtic knotwork hanging from the ceiling, they would have privacy in plenty.

In more ways than one their location couldn't be faulted. Their position overlooked a charming stone patio with a plethora of terracotta tubs filled with still abundant trailing pink and white blossoms, glinting in the pale light of late summer evening. It was breathtakingly pretty. The blooms surrounded a pretty fountain commanded by a modern sculpture.

Reluctantly withdrawing her admiring gaze from the appealing view, Ellie attempted to focus on the wine list the waiter had left them to peruse. Absently stroking the fine white linen napkin that had been draped on her lap, she fought hard against another intense desire to flee. And again she knew she would do no such thing. Whatever the consequences Nikolai intended, she would stay and face them.

If nothing else, Ellie was desperate to see Arina again. She was, after all, the closest link she had to her much loved sister, and now that her father's health was cause for concern she longed for the chance to somehow make amends and be part of her niece's life again. Ellie also wanted Nikolai to know that she wasn't about to follow the same escapist route she'd taken five years ago.

'Are you happy for me to select the wine?' he asked, civil-voiced and Ellie glanced back at him in surprise, not trusting the polite veneer.

'Go ahead,' she replied. 'I'm certainly no expert!'

'Maybe not with wine,' Nikolai commented smoothly. 'But clearly you have become an expert in psychology.'

'I may have got the necessary qualifications, but it takes a lifetime to be really expert at anything. And even then I'll still be learning! I mostly think of myself as an enabler…somebody who can help a person in trouble take the next step towards healing and hopefully give them some useful tools to help themselves.'

'Your humility is commendable…although your current high profile in the media is somewhat at odds with that, wouldn't you say?'

Having expected his derision at some point, Ellie wasn't disappointed now. Her whole body tensed. 'I'm not interested in having *any* sort of media profile, for your information! It only happened that I appeared on television because a local reporter where I worked got wind of a case I'd worked on and the client's father was well known.'

Nikolai named the politician concerned, with his trademark ice-cool equanimity, and Ellie grimaced. She might have known he would have all the information he needed at his fingertips.

'I have that reporter to thank for helping me locate *you,* so I cannot regret his interest!' he continued, with a faint ironic lift at the edges of his disturbingly sensuous mouth. 'A bottle of Château Lafite Rothschild will fit the bill perfectly to celebrate our timely little reunion, I think. The wine was named after a French politician, so perhaps it is fitting, yes?'

Knowing very little about wine, but silently concerned that it sounded frighteningly expensive, whatever it was, Ellie stayed mute.

'You need not look so overwhelmed!' her companion remarked in mock amusement. 'Naturally I will insist on footing the bill, so do not fret. The cost makes no difference to me. I have already expended too much time, money and concern over your whereabouts over the years as it is! I am only relieved that in the end my searching was not in vain! Tell me…why Scotland? Who did you know there? My informants certainly did not discover any extended family in that location, or anywhere else in the UK!'

His comments made Ellie revisit afresh the gravity of the horrific event that had changed her life for ever, and the devastation she had undoubtedly left behind her. As well as that came the disturbing realisation that Nikolai had not resumed his life in the way she'd hoped he would, forgetting all about her. For long moments she struggled to give voice to her racing thoughts.

'I don't know why. It's just a place like any other…a place where nobody knew us…where we could make a fresh start. My father was worried about me. That was why he took me away,' she finally explained.

'What was he worried about? That I would hold you

in some way responsible for what happened to my brother despite the verdict reached by the courts?'

The cold slash of Nikolai's chilling voice immobilised Ellie in her seat. Nervously she met the burning blue of his fiercely focused gaze, and it was like glancing into a frosted lake in deep midwinter.

'Well, he was right!' he spat out, laying down the wine list just as the soft-footed waiter returned to take their order.

Ordering the wine in a calmly controlled tone that was miraculously devoid of the rage he had just expressed, he told the man to give them a few extra minutes so that they could deliberate over the menu.

In the ensuing stomach-churning silence Ellie stared hard at the printed words in front of her in the leather-bound book, but they might have been written in Sanskrit for all the sense they made to her distracted gaze.

'Have you decided?' her stern-faced companion asked after less than a minute, the question sounding more like an impatient demand.

'A Caesar salad will be fine,' Ellie answered, hardly caring what she ate.

At a nod from Nikolai, another waiter peeled away from a nearby table and took their order. When they were alone again, Ellie set the menu aside and reached for the jug of water that was on the table, offering it to Nikolai first. He responded with a curt nod.

The barely contained animosity he emitted locked every muscle in her body with fear. Any threats this man made would not be empty ones, she knew. He had both the means and the will to make her suffer. *As if she had not suffered enough—and in ways he probably couldn't even begin to imagine...*

'How is—how is Arina?' Finally plucking up the courage to enquire about the one thing she was desperate to know most of all, Ellie knew her voice was barely above a whisper.

Nikolai's frozen glance did not thaw for even a second. 'Do you not think you relinquished the right to know that five years ago?'

'I never stopped caring about her...no matter what you might think!'

'But you obviously did not care enough, or you would not have deserted her like you did!'

'I didn't mean to just leave her like that. You make it sound like it was a pre-meditated decision, and it wasn't! I was hurt and traumatised from the accident, and for the first time in my life I let my father take charge and look after me. Was that so terrible? If you had seemed less closed-off and unapproachable, I would have talked to you about it... But—'

'What?'

'I knew you were hurting badly yourself...emotionally, I mean. You'd lost your brother...why wouldn't you be? I know what a loss like that is like. The last thing I expected was that you would want me to stay on and take care of Arina. How could we possibly co-exist under the same roof when it was clear that you hated me after what happened? Besides, I thought your wife might want to play more of a part in Arina's upbringing when I left.'

'Veronika and I are no longer married. We divorced not long after you disappeared.'

All the muscles in Nikolai's face seemed to freeze for a moment, and Ellie felt genuine shock ripple through her at his news.

'However I might have appeared,' he continued gravely, 'you should have put Arina's welfare first…not your own! You simply ran away—like the coward I now know you to be!'

The comment was like a sharp-bladed dagger plunged into Ellie's chest, and the pain that ensued took her breath away.

'I'm not a coward!' She slammed her hand down hard on the table and the glassware and crockery rattled. It felt as if every pair of eyes in the room was on her, but she was sick with misery and hurt at the unfairness of Nikolai's cruel remark.

She understood his need to vent—he must have been storing up resentment over the years, desperately needing someone to blame. But Ellie had suffered too.

'Is there no understanding or forgiveness in your heart at all?' she appealed. 'It's been five years, Nikolai! Do you honestly think it will help you come to terms with your grief any better by holding onto blame?'

It was the first time she had used his name, and she saw the flicker of surprise in his eyes.

'The answer to the first part of your question is no. There *is* no forgiveness in my heart where you are concerned, Elizabeth! I trusted you and you paid me back with nothing but deceit! You abandoned us…not caring what happened and clearly thinking only of your own position!'

Her stomach clamped in a vice of pain, Ellie glanced forlornly round at the other diners in the chic hotel restau-

rant, imagining she saw only pleasure and happiness reflected on their faces—states of mind that were a million
miles away from what *she* was currently experiencing.

Inhaling deeply, she turned back to Nikolai. 'How
did I deceive you? I only left because I was hurt and in
shock. Since when has that become a crime? And you're
wrong if you think I didn't care about what you and
Arina were going through. *Especially Arina*! There's
not a day that's gone by when I haven't wondered how
she is! I'm so, so sorry if I added to her suffering and
yours by going away. What more can I say?'

'You ask how you deceived me?' Nikolai drawled,
the low-pitched timbre of his arresting voice sending an
explosion of hot little shivers down Ellie's spine.
'Well…I will tell you. It is my belief that at the time of
the accident you were having an affair with my brother.'

'What?'

'Not only were you having an affair, but you were
also planning to elope with him—taking the baby with
you! It is my belief that is why you were in the car
together that day!'

'That's ludicrous!'

'Is it, Ellie?'

His unexpected use of the shortened version of her
name made Ellie stare at him for a suspended moment.
Then the adrenaline flooding her body after his unbelievable words kicked in, and she felt quite ill at the im-
plications that crowded in on her.

'How do you know?' Nikolai suggested with deadly
softness, his gaze making a dazed prisoner of hers.
'When you say you cannot remember anything? You

two always seemed pretty close, and what other reason would you have had for agreeing to drive him that day? If he had wanted to go somewhere alone he would have rung for a cab…not taken you with him!'

A small helpless groan left Ellie's throat, and she shook her head in frustration and misery at the yawning space in her mind where her memory should be. 'Look…I know I can't remember what happened that day, why I should have been in the car with him and Arina, but I'd swear on my life that your conclusion is a million miles away from the truth!'

The returning dark, condemning gaze on her companion's face said he didn't believe her, and Ellie's spirits sank even lower. No wonder he was furious with her if he thought that she'd been having an intimate relationship with his brother and planning to run away with him, taking the baby with them!

'And you're wrong about us being close. I offered Sasha comfort and support after my sister died, that's all! And after you suggested that I move into the Park Lane house and look after Arina full-time you *know* how infrequent his visits were. Sometimes he could be gone for weeks on end!'

'There is something else.'

Ellie hardly dared breathe.

'A valuable jewel was found in the wreckage of the car after the accident—a diamond necklace belonging to my mother that I kept in a locked casket in my bedroom. You must have heard Sasha arguing with me about money before I left to go to the office. Obviously it was stolen to help fund your new life together! Did the two of you plan the theft together, or was that something you decided on all by yourself?'

Laying her palms down on the fine linen tablecloth, Ellie desperately needed something to anchor her. All of a sudden her world felt like a wild storm-tossed sea, and she was drowning in it. Breathing out a harsh breath, she made herself look Nikolai straight in the eyes.

'Haven't you been listening to me at all? Sasha and I weren't having an affair, and I know nothing about any necklace being stolen! I know you won't believe me, because I can't prove it, but I *do* know my own nature—and I would cut off my hand before I took anything that wasn't mine from anybody!'

Nikolai shrugged. 'Unfortunately, Ellie, all the evidence seems to suggest that you *are* indeed guilty. It is not just the necklace. Other things went missing from the house around that time too. And the fact that you disappeared so suddenly after the inquest would make anyone suspicious! Your father must have known what you had planned, and he took you away so that you would escape punishment! Who knows? Perhaps he even helped you steal the necklace and those other things?'

'No! Is that why you searched for me?' Her voice was hoarse now, and Ellie's hand moved nervously against her throat. 'Because you wanted to prosecute me for theft as well as blame me for the accident?'

'If not you, Ellie…then your father! He has spent time in prison before for theft, has he not?'

The Russian sighed, as though it was all a mere formality, and Ellie's blood ran colder than any ice-packed river as she looked into that handsome, unforgiving face.

'What would you do in my position?' he asked. 'I have been both deceived and betrayed. Do you not think I deserve to be compensated in some way?'

'You can't involve my father! He's done nothing…I know he hasn't! And he's not a well man! Going to prison again would likely kill him!'

'How dramatic you are! I see there is indeed fire beneath that deceptively cool air you exude.'

'Don't mock me! If you're so set on accusing me of crimes I know nothing about let alone have participated in, and if you want compensation—then perhaps there is a way I can somehow pay you back? We should talk…work something out. I'll do anything as long as it doesn't involve my father! Please, Nikolai… Whatever you decide, leave him out of it!'

CHAPTER THREE

STUDYING the flawless buttermilk complexion of the lovely face before him, and steeling himself against her heartfelt plea, Nikolai sensed a renewed sting of fury and something perhaps equally disturbing but more personal sweep through him at the thought of Elizabeth with his brother.

Before he knew it, a blood-heating memory surfaced inside him, of an unforgettable encounter with her the day before the accident. It had been evening, the baby had long since been put to bed, and Nikolai had been looking over some important documents concerning a meeting he was due to attend the next afternoon. There was a lot of small print and equally as much red tape to wrestle with. Usually he didn't flinch for a second over such tasks, however tedious, but at that moment a world of onerous responsibility had weighed him down like an iron cloak across his shoulders, and he had longed to throw it off.

He had been groomed to take over his father's multi-million-pound oil empire when he should have been enjoying his youth—just as Sasha had been allowed to enjoy his. He had spent every minute of his day dealing with the complexities and demands of running a hugely successful business. All of a sudden the realisation had come to Nikolai that he was fatigued and disenchanted, and that the only thing he really longed for right then was his freedom… And not just from his sense of duty and responsibility. Veronika and he had barely been speaking to each other, and on the rare occasions when they were actually home at the same time lived in a state of near excruciating stalemate—neither of them having the time or energy to bring the increasingly brittle marriage to its deserved and grateful end. Nikolai had long suspected she might be seeing someone else.

Unexpectedly, Elizabeth had knocked on the door, shaking him out of his agonising introspection, and he had been grateful. She had brought him a cup of tea made just the way he liked it—black with sugar and lemon. When she had first arrived at the house to work he had been instantly drawn to her warmth and shyness, and her eagerness to learn new things. When she had exposed an interest, he had personally schooled her in the intricate art of making his favourite beverage in the highly deco-rated brass Samovar that had originated in Moscow and had belonged to Nikolai's great-great-grandmother.

Her thoughtful gesture in bringing him the tea, and the radiance of her presence, had acted like a soothing balm to Nikolai's soul, and he recalled smiling up at her with much more warmth than usual, his worries tempo-rarily forgotten. He remembered Elizabeth placing the mug carefully on the side of the desk, and how fascinated he'd suddenly become with the graceful contours of her small, pretty hand as she'd uncurled it from the porcelain. A powerful desire had consumed him to discover if the flawless texture fulfilled the idea of satin and silk, as its appearance so alluringly suggested.

Compelled by some irresistible force he hadn't been able to fight, Nikolai had reached out and cupped his palm over her knuckles, momentarily holding her captive. A bolt of electricity had harpooned through him like lightning, and Elizabeth had been equally affected. Her sweet breath had whispered over him like hushed gossamer silk, and Nikolai had gazed into her eyes and seen the same helplessly wild longing that he had known must blaze in his own hot glance.

'By all the saints!' Before he'd known it he'd been rising to his feet and cupping the back of her head, to free the pale ivory comb that confined her hair. It had fallen onto her shoulders like warm summer rain, drifting softly onto a sunlit meadow, and trickled through Nikolai's fingers like smooth, silken skeins of pure spun gold. He had caught his breath in sheer delight, the parameters of his world narrowing down to just the vision of her lovely face. His senses on fire, he had touched his lips to hers, finally drinking at the exquisite well that promised to satisfy his thirst and heal his wounds like no other…

Wrenching his mind free of the distracting and stirring memory, Nikolai forced himself to return to the present. The fact was—if his suspicions were correct—the lovely face and bewitching but treacherous lips before him had also been caressed by his brother, and it made him wonder if he had imagined the mutually hungry response and naked need in her eyes that day five years ago? Or was it simply that Ellie, as she called herself now, was a girl who took pleasure in teasing men with her beauty and sexuality just because she could?

Even though he had no evidence to support the idea, it was utterly distasteful to Nikolai's strong sense of male pride that she might employ such disingenuous behaviour—even once—and it completely doused the heat that had automatically flared inside him. But he knew that it would undoubtedly surface again. He had always been attracted to his brother's beautiful sister-in-law, and could no longer deny it. But he had been married when she had dropped out of college to come and take care of Arina after her sister's death.

Sasha had been in no fit state to take care of the baby himself, so had agreed to let Nikolai take charge of things. And, although there had been a definite maturity about the way Ellie had conducted herself, and also the way in which she'd taken care of her small charge, there had been a touching innocence about her too, and because of her comparative youth Nikolai had fought hard against his growing attraction for her.

'So—' he broke some bread between his fingers '—we will eat our meal and I will take some time afterwards to consider what kind of compensation I would like from you, Ellie.'

She pulled her gaze away from him, but not before Nikolai saw the tide of hot colour that rushed into her cheeks. Was it caused by anger, embarrassment, or something else? *Like that illicit kiss they had shared the evening before the accident*? His interest deepened.

'In the meantime…I'd like to see Arina,' she said, injecting a determined note into her soft voice.

Immediately Nikolai's fierce sense of protectiveness towards the little girl who had become his pride and joy surfaced, and he already knew his answer. 'That is not something I am going to agree to straight away—and I am sure you can guess at the reasons why. Arina is my daughter now. Yes…after Sasha died and Veronika and I split up I officially adopted her. After such an upsetting start in life she is happy and well-adjusted, and I am not about to jeopardise her happiness in any way—no matter how much you say you desire to see her again!'

'What do you think I'm going to do, Nikolai? Try and force her to accept me and like me?' Ellie's eyes were round with hurt. 'I didn't tell you before, but now that I've got used to the idea I'm *glad* that you found me! Yes—glad! I've wanted to see Arina for so long—even if it's only for a few minutes. She is my sister's only child, and I meant what I said when I told you I loved her and have never stopped loving her!'

'You will have to let me think about it. First of all I will need to see for myself the kind of person you have become in the years we have been apart, and whether you are indeed someone I would want involved in my daughter's life.'

'You make me sound like the very worst criminal!'

'Where Arina's well-being is concerned, I take no chances.'

'That's all I want, Nikolai.' Suddenly she looked close to tears. 'A chance! A chance to prove to you I'm neither a liar *or* a thief!'

'Trust has to be earned and built up... Especially when it has been shattered as badly as it has been in my case!'

The waiter brought the wine Nikolai had selected, and while the man expertly poured it into the waiting slim-stemmed glasses after his nod of approval he concentrated his gaze once more on the increasingly distressed expression on his beautiful companion's face. In a weak moment, Nikolai took pity on her.

'Arina has been at school full-time for about a year now—since she was five. She seems much enamoured with it.'

'Jackie always loved school... At least she coped with it much better than I ever did! How do you—how do you manage taking Arina and collecting her every day with your work commitments now that—now that your wife is no longer with you? Does she still have a nanny?'

'Between my housekeeper and my au pair we manage very well. Elsa—the au pair—is in charge of the school run, and Miriam—my housekeeper—also helps out when she is needed. Arina is fond of them both.'

'You have never—you've never thought about re-marrying?'

Ellie's question took Nikolai by surprise for a moment. After the soul-destroying relationship he had shared with Veronika he'd told himself he would avoid making a similar horrendous mistake again like the plague! Apart from occasionally thinking that Arina would benefit from having a mother in her life, he would not be human if he did not admit to feeling lonely from time to time too…lonely for a tender, loving woman who would not only warm his bed but would be a true partner in every sense of the word.

Women to warm his bed Nikolai could easily find… but someone tender and genuinely caring of his welfare…*that was another story entirely.*

'Not lately,' he replied, finally answering the question. 'But then I have preferred to devote my time and energy to taking care of Arina rather than invest it in a relationship. Besides, I have my work as well, and that also takes up a lot of my time.' He leaned forward a little across the table. 'What about you? Why are you still alone, Ellie?'

She bit down on her lip. 'How do you know I'm alone?'

'Because since I saw you on that television programme a month ago my sources have revealed that besides your father there is no one in your life… No one and nothing else to care about but your work!'

'You've had people checking up on me?'

'Under the circumstances I did what had to be done.'

Her returning glance was reproachful. Nikolai shrugged it off. It hardly mattered what she thought of his methods when she had treated him and Arina with little or no concern at all!

Taking a careful sip of his wine, he inclined his head approvingly. 'A good choice,' he remarked, allowing a corner of his mouth the briefest lift upwards. 'Even if I do say so myself!'

The man had a charismatic allure that would always

guarantee him plenty of female attention, Ellie mused somewhat resentfully. She was drawn like a magnet to the arrogant, almost autocratic set of features before her. Imaginative fantasies about what the hard, fit body beneath the expensive tailoring he wore would be like in bed would inevitably always be aroused too. And women would feel that same helpless pull towards him even if he was a pauper!

Ellie shivered as the familiar unbidden, disturbing fantasy stole into her mind…fuelled by her dizzying recollection of that kiss they had shared five years ago.

Having only been kissed once before by a boy at college—and pretty clumsily at that—nothing in the world could have prepared Ellie for the barely civilised and frightening passion of Nikolai's sizzling kiss. Even before his lips had made contact with hers, when he had simply covered her hand with his, an electrical bolt had shot through her insides and flooded her with the kind of heat more generally associated with the tropics. And when he had penetrated her mouth with his hot, silky tongue, Ellie had barely known how she remained standing.

She would have given him anything he'd asked for right then…anything…if only the telephone had not rung and shockingly broke them apart. Then guilt that he was married—and fear that taking things further would mean nothing to him—had sent her dashing from the room and back upstairs to her bedroom. To spend nearly the whole night lying awake, longing and wondering what it would be like to go to bed with the one man she had finally admitted she cared for and desired more than any other she had ever met…

But she had long ago given up on her impossible fantasy of being with Nikolai—and Ellie now sadly resigned herself to his hate and scorn instead.

'You study me very carefully beneath those eyes of green fire, Ellie.' His voice turned soft and beguiling all of a sudden. 'What do you see, I wonder? A wealthy, arrogant man who believes he can do anything he likes because money can open doors that remain firmly shut to those that do not have it?' He chuckled, amused at his own joke. 'Then you would be right. I cannot deny it!'

Ellie made no reply. She couldn't. Her throat was stinging to the point of pain, and she feared if she said anything emotion would overwhelm her. Bad enough to be accused of being somehow complicit in the car accident that had killed his brother, and of being his lover to boot, without knowing that this man—the one man she had secretly always admired and wanted—despised her and wouldn't even let her see her niece, her own flesh and blood, until she had somehow proved to him she was worthy of such a privilege! There was certainly no call for humour in the situation as far as she could see…unless of course it was of the blackest kind!

Plucking the starched white linen napkin from her lap, Ellie dropped it onto the table and rose determinedly to her feet. 'I'm sorry…but I suddenly don't feel very hungry any more.'

'Where do you think you are going? Sit down immediately!'

'I'm not a child! Don't you dare—'

'I said *sit down*!'

She froze at the undertone of menace in that deeply rich voice.

'Unless you want to risk making a scene—and very likely ruin your so far unblemished professional reputation for good—I would think very hard before you turn your back and walk away from me, Dr Lyons!'

Uncomfortably aware that they were already the unwelcome cynosure of several pairs of interested eyes, Ellie sank slowly back down into her seat. Right on cue the waiter appeared with their food.

'Perhaps when you start to eat you will find that you have an appetite after all? You are looking distinctly pale all of a sudden.'

'Can you wonder why?'

'No doubt it has been quite a shock to see me again, when you had obviously hoped to remain undetected by my radar for good.'

Withdrawing the angry retort that burned on her lips, Ellie forked some food into her mouth. Certain that she would be numb to any sensation of pleasure at all in what she ate, she was surprised to find that the crisp and bright Romaine lettuce, the anchovies and crunchy croutons, were really quite delicious. Her tastebuds responded with silent, hungry appreciation.

'This is good!' she remarked.

'Even the most average fare can taste like the best meal you have ever eaten when you are hungry.'

'I suppose in your world this food might be considered average, but I still say it's very good!'

'You were once a part of my world—remember?'

His lowered tone got her attention. Ellie laid down

her fork beside her plate. In the twelve months that she had lived in the Park Lane house looking after the baby, Nikolai had taken her to dine in some of the most exclusive restaurants in the world. Often they had been in places where he had fabulous homes—Long Island in New York, for instance, and Rome, Moscow and Monte Carlo, as well as here in London. Veronika had rarely accompanied them because her job as chief designer for a smart European fashion house had already entailed plenty of travelling.

Only in her heart of hearts had Ellie confessed to being glad about that. She had also noticed that Nikolai did not act as if he missed his wife…not at any time. Now she recalled that the opportunity to visit those fabulous locations and stay in the realms of such unmitigated luxury had been like a fantastic dream for a girl raised mainly in the fostercare system and sometimes in children's homes. But the way Nikolai now asserted she was once part of his world—as though he were suggesting she had meant something far more meaningful than someone who'd taken care of his niece—rubbed an already tender nerve raw.

'I was still just an employee of yours, even though we had a personal connection in Arina!' she exclaimed, the emotion she feared giving way to gripping her even more strongly.

'I treated you well, did I not?' His stunning azure gaze narrowed.

'Yes, you did. But—'

'What?''

She had been going to blurt out something about his

brother but, forcing herself to calm down, quickly thought better of it. There was still Arina to consider, and the poor child had surely suffered enough, being deprived of both natural parents, without Ellie bringing the taint of more painful shadows into her young life.

Shrugging unhappily, she tried to concentrate on her food, but her hunger had fled. Her serious-faced companion didn't seem to notice that she'd stopped eating.

'So…you still like children?' he said, dipping some bread into the fragrant carrot and coriander soup he had ordered.

'Of course!' His remark prompted an image of the adorable baby that had been her niece, and Ellie's heart swelled with longing. 'Won't you tell me a little about how Arina is now? What she looks like and her personality? I've tried so many times to imagine her, but…'

'She is mischievous, and full of life, but she has moments when she is just in a private little world all of her own. She has inherited my brother's dark colouring rather than your sister's fairer looks. Her hair is as black as treacle, and she has big blue eyes the colour of the sky—and already she has the boys in her class lining up for her attention!'

'A real heartbreaker, then?'

'Yes…a heartbreaker.'

Nikolai's smile broke across his face like the rising of the dawn following a grim black night, and hearing the love and pride in his voice, Ellie was helplessly moved. One thing that did stand out in her memory was his unwavering devotion to the little girl. He had loved her from the outset. How many other men in his demanding position would have taken on the serious lifelong responsibility of another man's child—even if that man *had* been his brother? Whatever his faults… nobody could criticise him for that.

Before she'd gone to work for Sasha and Nikolai, Ellie had experienced two previous jobs as a nanny— one for a doctor's family and the other for a couple who had both been solicitors. Her natural affection for children and her own desperate desire to somehow redress the balance of her own love-starved childhood had meant working as a nanny was the perfect job. But then Jackie had persuaded her to go to college and work towards getting a qualification in psychology—something Ellie's sister knew she had also yearned for.

When Nikolai had met her in the hospital just after Jackie's shocking death, and they had all discussed the baby's future and who was going to raise her, Ellie had had no hesitation in giving up her degree course to go and live in his house and take care of their niece. Sasha had all but gone completely to pieces, and Nikolai had instructed him to go away for a few weeks and try and get his head together.

At that first ever meeting with him Ellie had been quite overwhelmed by the handsome Russian. By the time she'd left that day—even though she'd been numb with grief and sadness over her sister—she hadn't been able to get his piercing blue eyes out of her mind. He'd suffered too, she'd seen. In spite of his staggering wealth and privileged position. Some great sadness had been walled up behind that unforgettable gaze, and Ellie had deduced again that outward appearances could be deceiving. She'd become adept at reading people and faces, and that was one of the reasons she had veered towards studying psychology—that and a heartfelt wish to somehow ease the mental and emotional suffering of others wherever she could…and try and understand herself too.

'She was just the loveliest baby to take care of!' she exclaimed now. 'I honestly can't wait to see her again.' Her suddenly self-conscious gaze met and held Nikolai's, and the smile that was like the dawn breaking vanished from his austere lips, as though he immediately regretted or even *resented* sharing it with her.

'What about having children of your own?' he asked gruffly. 'Have you ever thought about that?'

Ellie frowned. 'Yes…as a matter of fact I have. But for that to happen I'd have to be in a stable and loving relationship—I wouldn't bring a child into the world otherwise! Anyway…I don't think that's going to be on the cards for a long time yet. Right now I think I am needed much more elsewhere.'

'By your clients, you mean?'

'Yes.' Raising her glass of wine to her lips, she took a small conservative sip and placed it back down on the table. 'What about you?' she enquired of the man sitting opposite, her heart thudding nervously at her temerity in asking such a question. 'Would you like children?'

'As a matter of fact I would. Arina has brought more joy into my life than I ever thought possible and a brother or sister or both to join her would be very much desired. But…like you…that is not on the horizon for me right now. Now, let us continue with our meal, shall we?'

CHAPTER FOUR

UNABLE to stem his impatience as he waited for Ellie
to emerge from the television studios, Nikolai could
hardly believe he had let her out of his sight after they
had had dinner together last night. He still did not trust
her, but apart from forcibly detaining her or kidnapping
her, frankly what else could he have done?

At the back of his mind he supposed he still feared
that she'd flee again, but this time Nikolai had instructed Ivan his bodyguard to keep a watch on her
movements. So far she was exactly where she said
she'd be, but something else had been gnawing away
at him after their meeting. Thinking back to the events
that had led up to the car accident, he had reluctantly
started to acknowledge that he had played *his* part in
what had occurred that terrible day too. It was not an
easy admission to make. A man who prided himself on
making good decisions, that day Nikolai had made
what was probably the very *worst* decision of his life.
Sasha had been drinking heavily, and that was one of
the reasons they had rowed so bitterly. His brother had

also been demanding more money to fund his out of control and soulless lifestyle, as well as displaying his usual unbelievable indifference to his daughter's welfare.

In the year since he had lost Jackie, Sasha had failed to improve his life in any way…it had been as if he was hell-bent on destroying himself too. All things considered, Nikolai had certainly had plenty of reasons to be mad at him that day. But what he could not begin to fathom was how or why he had never suspected before that there might be something going on between him and Ellie—because that was the conclusion he had reached, and it would not go away. Why else would she have driven him that day, and risked getting into the most dreadful trouble when it had been Nikolai's car she was driving and he had warned his brother to stay put until he returned from his meeting?

If he had suspected that they were closer than he had thought then Nikolai never would have left the two of them alone together that afternoon. It had been vital that he get to his office for a crucial meeting, but he should have insisted that Ellie simply bring Arina and go with him. Not left her behind with the man she'd agreed to run away with, taking the baby with them! The meeting had been set up for Nikolai to formally present and then sign an employment contract that would guarantee the jobs of over one and a half thousand migrant workers in the city. He had not wanted to delay, as people's livelihoods depended on it, so Nikolai had reluctantly left Ellie and his niece alone with an already unstable Sasha, and hastened to his office to meet with his board and do what had to be done—telling himself that by the time he returned to Park Lane his brother might have calmed down sufficiently for Nikolai to be able to talk some sense into him.

Little had he known that by the time he got back Sasha would be dead and Ellie would be lying unconscious in an ambulance, on her way to hospital, with a kind policewoman comforting a sobbing and terrified but thank God *unhurt* Arina until they could reach Nikolai and tell him what had happened.

A tight band of tension squeezed his temples in a vice, and he briefly shut his eyes. When he opened them again he saw Ellie hurrying from the uninspiring redbrick building that housed the television studios towards him—her footsteps slowing the nearer she got to the car. She was wearing a red blazer, a white blouse and a knee-length black skirt with black hosiery. *Nikolai found himself fascinated by her slim and shapely legs.* For the first time since meeting up with her again he noticed that she walked with a slight limp. It was not something that everyone would immediately observe, but it was a limp just the same.

A wave of unexpected emotion crashed in on him. His hours of waiting by her hospital bedside for her to regain consciousness after the accident returned. Hours that had turned into days before—back in the land of the living—she had seemed to have forgotten who he was, and had just stared at him from time to time with a sad far-away look in her eyes—a melancholic gaze that even in his grief and rage over Sasha's death had somehow pierced his soul…

'Hi,' she greeted him a little breathlessly, as the electronic window beside Nikolai slid down. 'Sorry if I'm a bit later than I said. The director wanted a word with me.'

'Get in,' he replied, struggling to maintain his equilibrium, and unbalanced further by the strangely powerful effect of her summery perfume and her beautiful face.

'Where are we going?' The perfectly smooth skin on Ellie's brow tightened a little, as if she was fighting the urge to escape him after all.

'I am taking you to dinner. Where else did you think we were going?'

She flushed a little. 'I was hoping you might have relented and would let me see Arina,' she admitted softly.

'Not yet. We have still got some talking to do. How was your day at the studios?'

'All right.' She lifted her shoulders in a shrug.

Again, her scent arrowed acutely into Nikolai in an explosion of erotic sensuality, and it had the effect of tightening the iron muscles in his abdomen like a vice in his bid to stay immune.

'But the studio lights shining on me all day were too hot, and I felt like I was melting! It can make it pretty hard to think straight when I'm supposed to be giving people advice! It's definitely not an environment I would regularly like to work in.'

'I think a lot of young women would envy you the opportunity of being filmed and having the rest of the country watching you!'

'Because they crave their fifteen minutes of fame,

you mean? I wish I could tell them how empty that is! It means nothing. When the admiration and applause dies away you still have yourself to face!'

Silently, Nikolai agreed, and he felt a distinct surge of approval that she echoed his own feelings on the whole concept of fame and celebrity. As well as knowing the emptiness of it, he was also a person who relished his privacy, and whenever that was intruded upon by the press or the media in general he resented it mightily.

'So? What kind of food would you like to eat tonight? The choice is yours. We can go anywhere.'

'Must we go to another restaurant? I'm feeling rather tired tonight, and I would much rather eat at home. I can put together some pasta and a sauce, if that would suffice and you'd care to join me?'

Nikolai's eyebrows shot up in surprise. An invitation back to where Ellie lived had not featured in his thoughts at all. He'd believed that she was far too wary of him to put herself in such a potentially vulnerable position. Yet it was an opportunity that he would not hesitate to take advantage of. Since their conversation last night an idea had taken root in his mind and would not leave him. Considering it now, Nikolai thought that it would probably be better put to her in the confines of her own home rather than in a public place where anyone might eavesdrop.

'Pasta would be just fine,' he agreed. 'Tell me your address and I will instruct my chauffeur.'

When the car pulled up in the street outside where Ellie lived in London's East End, Nikolai, having observed the general area as they drove—the graffiti-scrawled hoardings, the rubbish littering the streets, the damaged cars and the air of neglect—told his chauffeur to leave. When the time came he would get a cab home, he declared.

He put his hand beneath Ellie's elbow as she opened her front door. It was not easy to shrug off the automatic urge to protect her from harm, even though she had caused him no end of turmoil and distress. Already knowing he hated the idea of her living in such a run-down and dangerous area, Nikolai wondered why she had chosen to make her home there.

Ellie refused to feel embarrassed about where she lived, or the fact that her tiny flat was not full of the things most people in the crazy consumer-ridden world they lived in knocked themselves out working to buy. Most of her furniture was second hand, but it didn't bother her one jot. The fact was her little home was clean and tidy and it was *hers*. When she finished work each day, after meeting the demands of clients and the people at the homeless shelter, it was a most welcome haven, and she never stopped being grateful for it.

'There's a hook behind the door if you want to hang your coat up,' she told Nikolai as breezily as she could manage, still shocked at herself for inviting him.

Briefly going into the living room, she threw her blazer onto the overstuffed striped sofa with its cheer-fully displayed cushions, then made her way back out into the long galley kitchen to start cooking. Kicking off her shoes with a heartfelt sigh, she was more than glad to feel the cool wooden floorboards beneath her hot and tired feet. But suddenly every muscle in her body stiffened at the sight of the charismatic man who came and stood in the doorway. For a stunning moment he regarded Ellie with something that she momentarily fooled herself might be warmth. *Why had she invited him here, into the one place that she truly felt safe?* His presence compromised that feeling of safety more than anything else in her world right now.

Reaching for the tall glass jar of dried spaghetti in an overhead cupboard, she felt her throat lock in sudden anguish. She so wanted him to see that she was good…decent…not someone he should revile. She was a person who could be trusted…a caring aunt whose greatest wish in the world was to be able to see her deceased sister's child again… Maybe while he was here, Ellie could at last convince him of that?

Upstairs in a bedroom drawer, she had a small pile of birthday and Christmas cards, notes and letters she had written to Arina over the years. But she had never plucked up the courage to send them in case Nikolai merely destroyed them.

'Do you want a drink while I'm cooking?' she asked. 'If you open the fridge there's a bottle of white wine in there.'

Nikolai fetched the wine without replying, and as he did so Ellie placed two small glasses on the worktop. 'It's a screw top,' she told him over her shoulder as he studied the label on the bottle, 'so you don't need an opener.' She flinched. She couldn't help it. She was pretty certain that Nikolai had *never* drunk wine from a bottle without a cork—let alone one that wasn't vintage or expensive.

'Can I do anything to help?' His gaze moved interestedly round the kitchen, skimming the calendar with its scenic view of Lake Derwent in the Lake District, the large antique clock with Roman numerals that Ellie had bought from a local flea market, and the fridge magnets with warm-hearted sayings that she was in complete agreement with. His focus swiftly returned to his companion.

Could he help? Such an idea was so incongruous that Ellie couldn't help but display her amusement.

Nikolai's dark blond brows came together in a genuinely perplexed frown. 'What is so funny?'

'I suppose I just don't see you as someone domesticated…that's all.' Her smile was gently teasing. 'Wealthy businessman and all that.' But Nikolai stared back at her without commenting, merely looking at her as if he might never stop. To cover her embarrassment Ellie grabbed the bottle of wine and poured some into both glasses. She lifted hers straight away. 'Cheers!'

'I can cook and clean just as well as the next man,' he remarked wryly at last, the devastating blue eyes alight with unexpected humour. 'I can even make beds if the situation calls for it!'

Of all the domestic tasks he could have listed to illustrate his point, why had he picked *that* one? Ellie wondered, panicked, feeling her face flame. 'Then you'll make some lucky woman very happy one day, I'm sure!'

'You would settle for that, Ellie?'

Suddenly Nikolai was behind her, his warm breath lifting the fine tiny hairs at the nape of her neck and shockingly making her nipples prickle inside her bra and grow tight. Her whole body went rigid as a statue.

'You would settle for a man who would help you in the house...cook, clean and...make beds? I think I can offer you a little more than that!'

Confused by the announcement, as well as shocked by his nearness, Ellie spun round. 'What are you talking about?'

'Why not prepare the food and we will talk after dinner?'

'I want to talk now! What did you mean, Nikolai?'

His features inscrutable, he reached past her for his glass of wine. '*After* dinner,' he insisted.

Again Ellie found herself in a position where she could barely eat a thing. Her mind could hardly fathom his odd remark, and her anxiety round him increased.

After making a good job of eating the spaghetti with tomato and basil sauce she had made, Nikolai suggested they move into the living room, where they could be more comfortable, Ellie reluctantly led the way, speculating worriedly about what would take place next, and able to do little about the wild hammering of her heart. Remaining silent as she switched on the lamps and closed the curtains against the encroaching night, Nikolai elected to remain standing when Ellie sat down on the edge of the comfortable couch.

'Remember we talked yesterday about how you might compensate me for what happened?' he began.

All she could do was stare apprehensively.

'Well, I have come up with a way. You want to see Arina and be in her life again...yes?'

Ellie jerked her head in the affirmative, but still said nothing. She was waiting. Waiting to see just what form this *compensation* Nikolai talked about would take before considering the fall-out. *She was pretty sure there would be fall-out.*

'Well…there is a way in which you can see her each and every day, Ellie,' he continued gravely, all humour long gone from his spectacular blue eyes. 'You can agree to become my wife and return to Park Lane to live with us.'

There were some occasions in life when someone spoke words that elicited such monumental shock that you were struck speechless. For Ellie, *this* was one of those moments. The hands that had been previously folded calmly in her lap moved restlessly down to her sides, and she smoothed them nervously across the silky cotton mix of her skirt in a bid to steady them.

'This is the way you want me to compensate you?' she heard herself ask, her voice sounding strangely like someone else's. 'By becoming your *wife*?'

'Yes.' Sounding abrupt, Nikolai moved across the room to the bay window, lifted an edge of the plain cream curtain and briefly peered outside. Not too far away someone brashly honked a car horn, and the sound splintered through the silence of the room like breaking glass.

Turning back to Ellie, his features were full of foreboding, even in the soft glow of lamplight. *He was suggesting that she become his wife and yet he looked like he was going to the guillotine*, she thought unhappily, her stomach churning sickeningly.

'It will, of course, only be a marriage of convenience. I think you must already guess that?'

'Let me try and get this straight.' Rising to her feet, Ellie garnered all the dignity and courage she could muster to face him. 'Are you saying that the only way I get to see Arina again and be in her life is if I agree to this—this "marriage of convenience" with you?'

'That is correct. I have been thinking for some time now that Arina needs a mother, and as I have no one in my life at the moment to fulfil that role, and indeed am in no hurry to enter again into the state of matrimony for any other reason than that of convenience, after already having one failed marriage behind me, it would seem the ideal thing for me to do is to make you my wife, Elizabeth.'

By the mere fact he had referred to her by her original name—the name by which he had known her and then come to *despise* her—Ellie knew Nikolai was deadly serious about what he was proposing. Her heart seemed to crash into her ribcage in alarm and distress.

'But you don't even like me!' she declared, emerald eyes sparkling with helpless tears.

'It hardly matters.' The broad shoulders lifted carelessly. 'Seeing as this will not be a marriage that has come about by the normal route of most such liaisons. It is purely a business arrangement. The point is that you were always good with Arina…and you can be again. Of that I have no doubt. Only this time you will sign a binding contract that you will keep to this agreement of ours and not renege on it. If you try, then I will make sure you will rue the day that you were born, Elizabeth Barnes!'

'Ellie,' she answered defiantly, lifting her chin and inwardly recoiling at such a threat. 'I'm Ellie Lyons now, and I answer to no one but myself!'

Nikolai's mouth twitched in amusement. 'But soon you will be Mrs Golitsyn, and then you will answer to *me*!" he declared, taking no little satisfaction at the thought.

'And if I refuse to marry you?'

'Then you will never see or get the chance to speak to Arina again.'

'You can't do that! She's my sister's only child!'

'Watch me.' Nikolai's mouth was grim. 'Refuse this marriage, Ellie, and risk the consequences of me bringing a private case against you for the death of my brother and the attempted theft of the necklace and other items that disappeared—or marry me and achieve the closeness with Arina that you say you have long craved. The choice is yours.'

'What am I supposed to—?'

'I will give you twenty-four hours to make up your mind. If you agree, then we will discuss the terms of the marriage in more depth. If not...' His glance flicked over Ellie as if she would be beneath his contempt if she chose the latter route.

'And if I do agree...when can I see Arina?' Ellie already knew she had no other option but to accept Nikolai's unconventional proposal, even though it flooded her with many real fears and concerns.

Right at that moment she would not allow her mind to explore too closely what it would mean for her personally. Later, when she was alone, she would think about that. All she knew was that she had already missed out on five years of her niece's life, and she had no intention of missing out on the rest of it because of the bitterness of the man that had now become her father. She *owed* it to Jackie to do this.

Suddenly she admitted frankly to herself what had really prompted her return to London last year. It hadn't just been the opportunity to work there...Arina had always been on her mind, and in her heart, and more than anything else Ellie had been hoping against hope to see her again...

CHAPTER FIVE

IN THE cab on the way home last night, after he had left Ellie, Nikolai had reached another major decision. *He had decided to let her see Arina.* He was fairly certain that once she had set eyes on her sister's child again it would be practically impossible for her to refuse the marriage of convenience he had suggested. But Nikolai had a hidden agenda. Suddenly…*shockingly*…since spending time with her again he'd found himself impatient to make Ellie his wife.

Of all the women he could desire, want, need…*she* was the one who crowded thoughts of any others out. It hardly made sense to him, believing as he did that she had betrayed him with his brother and risked both his life and Arina's by driving the car that day, but Nikolai could not deny to himself what he felt.

When she came out of the television studios that afternoon he was waiting for her, with the declaration that he was taking her home to see her niece. Her bewitching emerald eyes swam with tears, but she quickly wiped them away and got into the car, simply murmuring 'thank you' and after that falling silent.

Electing not to say very much himself on the short journey to the house in Park Lane, Nikolai dwelt on the upcoming meeting between his daughter and her aunt, her former nanny, instead. They would clearly all need time to adjust to the new situation he was proposing, but he prayed that Arina would quickly learn to accept Ellie as her new mother once they were married, and as a result grow more confident with a more permanent female influence in her life.

His daughter's happiness meant everything to him. And even if it meant that for him there would never be the prospect of truly falling in love with a woman again—he was willing to make that sacrifice to guarantee his daughter's well-being.

Turning his focus to the plan he was devising for Ellie's long-term presence in their lives, he told himself it was only right that she should sacrifice some of the freedom she had stolen to pursue her chosen career when the child she had deserted had needlessly suffered because of her. *And it wouldn't be for ever…*just until Arina had left home and was forging a life of her own. After that Ellie and Nikolai could go their separate ways…

As his chauffeur steered the car into a waiting space in front of the elegant Park Lane residence, Nikolai turned to the woman at his side. She was not quick enough to hide the anxiety in her eyes, but he swiftly banished any treacherous urge to be sympathetic. 'She is just like any other normal healthy six-year-old girl,' he heard himself explain tersely. 'But obviously we will all have to take things one step at a time.'

A delicate frown creased Ellie's smooth brow. 'I'm not expecting her to accept me on sight! Relationships take time to build.'

'Good.'

'I just want to do what's right for her.'

'Then in that case…our aims are in perfect concord.'

It was impossible for Nikolai to keep the brusque tone from his voice. There were simply too many charged and chaotic emotions coursing through his blood for calmness to be a remotely viable option…

Inside the marble-floored hallway, Ellie met the privileged and wealthy air of her surroundings with a bittersweet upsurge of both happy and painful recollection. For long moments she was battered by emotion. Aware that Nikolai's steely-eyed gaze barely left her, she took a deep breath and grimaced. 'Everything is just the same as I remember it.'

'It was only six months ago that I had the place completely refurbished.'

'The décor may have changed, but the house itself feels just the same to me.'

'Then you must have a good memory after all, Ellie. I was quite certain it was a case of out of sight and out of mind as far as we were concerned!'

His imperious gaze mocked her mercilessly, and Ellie experienced a strong urge to get this daunting and emotional reunion over with as soon as possible. Not because she didn't want to see Arina—she was *desperate* to do so, and had been quite overwhelmed when

Nikolai had turned up at the studios and told her where he was taking her. But his unforgiving and punishing attitude towards her was seriously beginning to get to her. Did he imagine that Ellie had no feelings at all about entering this house again? Did it never even cross his mind for one moment to realise that it was as difficult for her to confront the past as it was for him?

'I haven't forgotten anything about my time here.' She lifted her chin. 'Up until the accident I was very happy here, and contrary to what you might believe I haven't concocted some convenient story about losing my memory to escape whatever retribution you think I deserve! I genuinely have no recall of what happened that day.'

'That is a topic of discussion for another more appropriate time, I think. Right now it is Arina who should be our first concern. Follow me. It is almost her bedtime, and at this time of the day she will probably be playing with her toys or listening to a story read by Elsa…the au pair,' he explained.

Walking behind Nikolai's tall, straight-backed figure up the grand sweeping staircase, with its sumptuous carpeted tread and Georgian elegance, Ellie didn't have a hope of calming the nerves that seized her. Everything was simply too raw…too achingly familiar and affecting for the skills in psychology she had painstakingly acquired over the years to be of any use to her whatsoever.

Moving in silence down a corridor lined with beautiful and expensive art, they stopped outside a once familiar door. Ellie's insides clenched hard, but without saying a word to her—as if any thoughts or feelings she might have were totally irrelevant to him—Nikolai rapped smartly on the cream painted oak and opened the door. Inside a large bedroom that was a little girl's dream, a small, pretty dark-haired girl sat on an exquisite hand-made bed, beautifully decorated with fairy princess imagery and a lilac and white quilted bedspread. Next to her sat a kind faced, big-boned young woman, with smiling brown eyes and sandy-coloured hair.

She immediately got up when Nikolai and Ellie entered, her smile open and generous. She seemed genuinely pleased to see them both. 'Welcome, welcome! And how are you today?' Her accent was definitely from one of the Scandinavian countries. 'We have just been reading one of Arina's favourite stories...*The Princess and the Pea*!'

She beamed, and Ellie sensed herself immediately warming to Arina's au pair. Nikolai's attention had immediately been captured by the child who was busy launching herself off the low-sided bed into his waiting arms.

'Papa!'

Ellie sensed tears prick the backs of her eyelids. Seeing the child was a double-edged sword for her. First of all she was poignantly reminded of the beautiful baby she had loved as if she were her own, and whose growing-up years she had sadly missed because of her flight to Scotland. And second the shocking realisation hit her that the six-year old Arina was a perfect miniature of Sasha, with her big china-blue eyes and rich dark hair. There was very little resemblance to her beloved sister Jackie at all.

The younger Golitsyn brother had looked like a hero from some ancient folk tale, with his lustrous dark locks and ethereal light blue eyes. The pity was that his addictions had started to take their toll on his remarkable good-looks, and taint the charm that had always drawn others so effortlessly into his sphere. *Something that Ellie knew to her cost.*

Now, watching Nikolai swing the little girl up into his arms and kiss her soundly on both cheeks, she was struck by what a breathtaking picture of unity and happiness they made together, and an inexplicable pang of loneliness and envy went through her. Addressing his daughter in Russian, Ellie heard him mention her name—it seemed that he had decided to stick with Ellie and not Elizabeth after all. Returning the child to her feet, he scraped his fingers through the regimented short thick strands of his dark blond hair and smiled—simply because he couldn't seem to help himself.

The sculpted features that already had the power to command instant attention wherever he went, because they were so striking, lit up even more when backed by the inner glow of pure pleasure behind them, Ellie discovered—and she couldn't help but stare.

'Ellie used to look after you when you were very small, Arina…just a baby. Say hello.'

'Hello.'

The big blue eyes moved up and down and all over her as if noting every facet and detail of Ellie's appearance and storing it to memory. Finally, she grinned, and hopped from one foot to the other—clearly pleased with what she'd discovered.

'You look just like a fairy princess!'

'That's just what I was going to say about you!' Ellie

replied, stooping low so that she would be on the same level as the little girl. Gently she touched the tips of her fingers to the child's silky-soft pink-bloomed cheek and felt something inside her—some psychic bond of love that had never been broken—leap for joy. 'In fact, I think you must be the prettiest fairy princess I've ever seen—especially as you have the loveliest black hair... just like Snow White!'

'I like that story,' Arina solemnly replied, then leaned towards Ellie and confided, 'But I like the story about Cinderella better! I don't like the way her ugly sisters were so horrible to her. Papa says they were jealous because Cinderella was kind and beautiful and they were ugly and mean and wanted to marry the prince— but in the end he married Cinderella and they lived happily ever after!'

'What a sensible prince! I think he made the right choice, don't you? And I do so like happy endings!' Ellie smiled.

'Then maybe one day *you'll* meet a handsome prince and live happily ever after too!' came the child's ingenuous reply.

Feeling Nikolai's azure-blue gaze burn with a deep blue flame as he silently observed her, Ellie went hot and cold all over. There would be no happy ending for her in this mockery of a marriage she was being forced to contemplate...she knew that. And suddenly along with that painful realisation came the knowledge that her work helping others have better relationships—with themselves, with others—would be all she could ever really hope for in that area. Even in her own opinion she was simply too messed-up ever to sustain a long-term relationship with any man.

She had been abandoned by her father and had her faith in men compromised by her sister's widowed husband, and now there was this intimidating proposal of marriage from Nikolai. How was she supposed to feel confident in *any* potentially intimate relationship with a man? Her faith and trust had been shattered and her self-esteem demoralised.

Slowly she rose to her feet, unable to resist ruffling the top of Arina's silky dark head as she did so. The child was gorgeous, and already Ellie knew she had the kind of naturally sweet temperament that would melt even the hardest heart. *She was a daughter any mother would be proud of...*

'That is another thing about Arina.' Bending his head, Nikolai captured his daughter's hand and kissed it extravagantly. 'She is one of life's optimists! She always looks on the bright side. Don't you, my angel?'

'Did you really look after me when I was a baby?' The child turned a curious long-lashed gaze back to Ellie.

'I did, sweetheart.' Pursing her lips, Ellie wanted to smile back—but emotion locked her throat painfully tight, and she didn't want to display what she was sure Nikolai would only see as another undesirable flaw in her character if she should suddenly give way to tears.

'Why didn't you stay with me? Did you get fed up with me?'

The question stunned Ellie. Looking to Nikolai for help was futile when all he was intent on doing was watching *her* constantly—as if waiting for her to somehow trip up and further prove his negative opinions about her.

Ignoring him, she dropped back down to the child's level and folded her hand carefully in her own. 'Of course I didn't, darling! You were the most adorable, wonderful baby that ever was, and I was so sad when I had to leave you. But I was in an accident, and…' She glanced up at Nikolai and silently he shook his head, indicating that his daughter knew nothing about the car accident and that Ellie was not to elaborate. 'I got hurt, and I was in hospital for a while. Afterwards my father took me away so that I could properly get better. But I missed you so much when I left, and I thought about you all the time!'

'And now you have come back!' The child's smile was huge…as if to say *that's sorted, let's get onto something else!* Pulling her hand free, she danced across the room back to Elsa. 'Can we finish my story, please?' she begged, her father and Ellie more or less forgotten.

'Why, of course! But then you have to brush your teeth and get ready for bed, because you have to get up for school in the morning!'

'We will leave.' Moving across the room to kiss his daughter an affectionate goodnight, Nikolai turned back to Ellie. 'I think it is time for us to go and have dinner.'

'I didn't realise you expected me to stay and eat with you.'

'You need to eat, I need to eat…of course you will stay to eat dinner! We also have some important business to complete…yes?'

* * *

Dinner was a fairly tense affair, with Nikolai at one end of the grand highly polished dining table, in the dining room with its stately windows overlooking the well-tended and manicured garden, and Ellie at the other. After his initial enquiries as to what she thought of Arina after not seeing her all this time it seemed her host was not disposed to make conversation.

It was obvious that some deep contemplation about the situation was preoccupying him, and Ellie could not really attest to minding the silence that descended between them. She was thinking hard too. Mostly wrapped up in the memories she did recall of her time in the Golitsyn household—she was quite relieved to let the time drift by with no mention of the marriage of convenience Nikolai was proposing. She knew it was only a temporary reprieve from what was looking more and more inevitable, but strangely, after a sleepless night contemplating it, and now after seeing Arina, some of her apprehension was calming down.

When Miriam brought them their coffee at the end of the meal, Nikolai suggested they take it into the drawing room. Finding herself alone with him after the attentive presence of his housekeeper and the young maid who had been helping to serve the meal, Ellie glanced round her and saw the exquisitely appointed drawing room had indeed been refurbished since she had seen it last. With its original Georgian box sash windows and sumptuous velvet drapes, it took the words 'elegance' and 'good taste' to a whole new level. Visually, it was absolutely stunning. It was a room in which to have tea in the very best fine bone china, amidst a backdrop of ever so polite conversation, Ellie decided privately. It definitely wasn't the kind of space where you could just throw down some comfy cushions on the floor and chill out, watching your favourite programme on TV!

Not that she could ever imagine a man like Nikolai indulging in such a commonplace pastime! He was a man made for more high-class pleasures...like fine wines, the best restaurants, and yachts in the South of France. He would most likely scorn the simple pursuits that interested Ellie.

Sighing, she let her gaze move round the room some more. With its innovative mix of contemporary and vintage furniture, and desirable art decorating the walls, it made Ellie's little flat in Hackney resemble some kind of hermit's retreat! However, the notion of envy didn't enter her mind for even a second. At this point in her life she was merely grateful to be alive and doing a job she truly loved—a job where she had a real opportunity to make a difference to young people's lives. Compared to that, Nikolai's beautiful house and staggering wealth hardly even signified.

'I'm going to have a cognac with my coffee,' he announced, interrupting her thoughts with the smoky gravel-edged tones of his compelling voice. 'What about you?' Pulling his silk tie free of his pristine shirt collar, he moved across to the burr walnut cocktail cabinet and opened it.

'Nothing for me, thank you.'

'Why not?' He raised a quizzical eyebrow.

'Because I need to try and get a good night's sleep,

and alcohol doesn't really help me do that. I'm working with two new clients for the TV programme and I need to keep a clear head.'

'One small cognac will not hurt. You look like you could use a drink to put some colour back into those pale cheeks of yours!'

Knowing the colour always seemed to drain out of her whenever she was tired, but surprised that he had noticed, Ellie shrugged. 'Okay… Just a small one, then.'

'So…did seeing Arina again fulfil your expectations?' After handing her a crystal goblet-shaped glass, the amber liquid inside it glistening in the subdued lighting of the various elegant lamps dotted round the room, Nikolai went and stood by the white marble mantelpiece that was above the stunning fireplace—every inch the Lord and Master of all he surveyed.

From her position on the supremely comfortable sofa, Ellie breathed a small sigh of relief that he hadn't joined her. 'It was the strangest experience… All this time apart and yet everything about her felt so familiar…as though I'd never left at all.' She shook her head in wonder. 'I thought she was adorable and beautiful! She's grown into the loveliest child, Nikolai!'

'I agree. Nobody would guess that her early beginnings were less than they should have been. My only wish now is that she will grow up into a happy and well-adjusted young woman. To achieve this, I have long realised, a girl should have a mother as well as a father. That is where you come in, Ellie.'

Hardly knowing what to say, Ellie fell silent. What he was proposing set her heart racing, and she tried to imagine what her life would be like living on such intimate terms with a man like Nikolai Golitsyn. The word 'intimate' conjured up particular dread for her, and she prayed that this 'convenient' marriage he was set on would not include what were her very worst fears. Surely he would find some other 'means' of satisfying that aspect of things without involving her? she thought, panicked. *But her heart was torn with a longing that contradicted that hope.*

Lifting her gaze, she found herself yet again under the ever-watchful surveillance of those azure-blue eyes. Had he guessed what was going through her mind just then? Her cheeks burned like a brand at the idea that he had. Self-consciously adjusting her position on the sumptuous sofa, Ellie took a tentative sip of her cognac. Its searing warmth had an immediate effect, and she sensed her cheeks tingle with even more heated colour. She made a mental note not to drink any more.

'From what I gleaned after the way you looked at me upstairs, when I mentioned being hurt in an accident, I gather that you haven't spoken to Arina about what happened?'

'No, and I do not intend to until she is much older! Thankfully she remembers nothing of that day, because she was too young. She only knows that her father died, and so far she has not asked me why.'

'What about her mother? Has she asked about her?'

'She knows that Jackie died giving birth to her, and that that was when you came to the house to live with us and help take care of her.'

'And what about the fact that I'm her aunt, Nikolai?

Did you tell her that? Or am I supposed to keep quiet about that and act as if I am just a stranger who came to look after her when her mother died?'

'I will tell her soon who you really are. Like I said before…we need to take things one step at a time.'

The fierce look in his eyes reminded Ellie of a proud male lion defending its offspring against predatory hunters, and she flinched at the evidence of reluctance in his voice. It was further proof of his lack of trust in her, and Ellie couldn't deny that hurt. Yet beneath her pain was the steadily growing vow that she would show him that she *could* be trusted—would strive daily to prove it.

'Nikolai? I loved seeing Arina again, and the idea of becoming her mother… Well…it's an overwhelming privilege, as well as the greatest responsibility! And perhaps the very *least* I could do, considering her mother was my sister. But when it comes down to the reality of the situation, I really think this idea of yours about us getting married and me living with you couldn't possibly work!'

'One can make anything work if one is committed and dedicated to the task, Ellie.'

Nikolai moved across the room to stand in front of her, and his sudden close proximity and the disturbing clean sharp scent of his expensive cologne made Ellie's muscles go rigid with tension. Glancing up at him, she saw he really was quite formidable right then.

'And seeing the way that Arina responded to you even after all these years has convinced me that what I am proposing is absolutely right! If you do not make up your mind to do as I ask then you leave me no choice but to start legal proceedings against you! Do not make the foolish mistake of imagining I will not follow through with what I say, Ellie. I am completely serious about this!'

CHAPTER SIX

'IF I DO agree to the marriage...what are the terms?' Quietly and with dignity, Ellie fearlessly met Nikolai's frosty gaze.

Inwardly he sensed something settle, and realised he had all but been holding his breath, waiting for her answer. Moving back across the room, he resumed his position in front of the fireplace.

'The main one would be that you agree to remain my wife until Arina is grown—shall we say twenty-one? After that we can divorce. You may leave my household, but you will remain her mother...agreed?'

'I would hardly want to bring *that* relationship to an end!' Ellie frowned and took what looked to be a reluctant sip of her cognac. 'What about my work and my commitments to people?'

'You may still pursue your career, with all that that entails—including your commitments to those people who have come to rely on you. I suppose you are mainly referring to your father? But Arina's needs must always come first. For instance, if she is ill I would expect you to stay and look after her, *not* the au pair or my house-keeper. The nature of my own work will also entail you accompanying me and Arina on essential trips abroad from time to time. I have become accustomed over the years to taking her with me whenever I go away—especially if it is a long trip—and she too has come to expect that. As she gets older I will hire a private tutor to school her whenever we are out of the country, so she will not miss out on her education.'

'Your expectations as far as me being a mother to Arina are not unreasonable, Nikolai, but I would expect some degree of flexibility from you as regards my work. For instance, when someone is having ongoing coun-selling it could be extremely disruptive for me to go away indefinitely…not to mention distressing to my client.'

'Then when the situation arises we will negotiate for the best interests of all concerned. I am not an ogre, Ellie…even though you may think me hard-hearted and unforgiving. I can be reasonable too.'

He allowed himself the smallest of conciliatory smiles, but Ellie did not look particularly convinced by it. *Would she resent him for good, given that he was more or less forcing her into this marriage*? This time Nikolai *did* harden his heart. He was only demanding what was owed to him *and* Arina, he reminded himself. Once he saw that Ellie was as good as her word in being the kind of mother to their daughter he expected then bit by bit she would come to see that there were defi-nitely certain benefits to being married to a man of his considerable wealth and position. Benefits that would surely more than make up for what she might regard as her perceived lack of freedom?

'There is one more thing I have to ask.' Placing her glass on the nearby walnut side table, Ellie rose to her feet.

Where her cheeks had appeared pale before, there was now evidence of a definite rose coloured tint in them. But beneath her lovely eyes were also visible signs of strain and tiredness. Remembering she had said that she'd struggled beneath the hot studio lights all day, Nikolai frowned.

'Go on,' he said, folding his arms across his chest.

'There's no delicate way to put this, so I'll just have to come right out and say it.'

The rose-pink in her cheeks deepened almost to scarlet, and Nikolai felt a tug of intrigue and…yes…a quiet excitement deep in his belly. He had already easily guessed the nature of her tentatively voiced question, because the subject had inevitably been on his mind too.

'Are you expecting us to be intimate once we are married?'

'I have the same needs as any other red-blooded male, Ellie,' he heard himself answer nonchalantly. 'And as a woman no doubt you must share similar needs. So my reply to your question is yes…I think being intimate will be a natural consequence of us living together, and may even make the marriage better than we could have hoped for!'

Her emerald-eyed glance should have spoken volumes as to her feelings, but right then Nikolai was so captivated by their beauty and luminosity he lost the capacity to think about what else was going on. But inside he did sense a thrill of anticipation at the idea of making love to her. *Something he had long craved since that explosive kiss they had shared all those years ago…*

'I would also like you to move in *before* we are married,' he announced, still gazing directly into her eyes. 'It will give us both a chance to adjust to the new situation, as well as getting Arina used to the idea that we will soon be wed.'

'What about my flat? I can't just leave it and not go back!' Ellie focused determinedly on the less sensitive of his proposals.

'Do you own it?'

Ellie flushed. 'I have a mortgage—like most people.'

'Then I would suggest you either make arrangements for someone to rent it or else put it on the market to sell. Let me know what you decide and I will take care of it for you if you like.'

He saw her swallow and look away.

'It seems like you've thought of everything!'

'I am accustomed to sorting things out. It is not a problem. Do you agree to my terms regarding the marriage?'

'I want to see Arina regularly and be a part of her life again, and after all this time apart from her I don't want to jeopardise that… So, yes…I agree to the terms, Nikolai.' She agreed even as the thought of their proposed intimacy danced around in her head. 'It all feels a bit unreal to me at the moment, but I expect I will eventually get used to what's happening. Now that we've discussed things…I'd really like to just go home and be by myself for a while. It's been quite a day, one way and another.'

Relieved beyond measure by her reply, Nikolai sighed and briefly moved his head in agreement to her request.

Shortly afterwards, having assured Ellie that he would be in contact again the following day, he allowed her to leave and his chauffeur took her home.

Nursing what remained of his cognac, Nikolai went to sit on the sofa in the same spot that she had occupied only minutes before. Shutting his eyes, he knew every sense he possessed was alert to not just the summery perfume that lingered there, but also to the disturbingly feminine essence Ellie had left behind her. Ellie… Mrs Elizabeth Golitsyn.

Smiling with possessive satisfaction, Nikolai opened his eyes again. He had taken the first vital step in achieving what he now knew he desired above all else—a convenient union between them, with his daughter's happiness and security paramount. He told himself he should be more than pleased. However, he had not been immune to the doubt and reluctance in the beautiful emerald eyes that had pierced him after Ellie had agreed to the marriage and his terms, and it had been a harsh pill to swallow. She had cared for his brother, *not* him! he savagely reminded himself—plus, he was black-mailing her into a marriage she did not want. Why *should* she be remotely pleased?

Both thoughts cut into him like Damascus steel, and he swallowed down the rest of his drink with little pleasure, grimacing at the fire that erupted inside his stomach. As long as Ellie kept her word and made Arina her priority then Nikolai told himself he could bear her disturbing presence. Indeed, this marriage of theirs would have compensations as well as convenience. Ellie was now perfectly aware that he expected her to share his bed, and had not even put up an argument.

Telling himself that she was at least being honest about that aspect of her nature, and would not want to contemplate a union with a man *without* sex, Nikolai pushed to his feet and depressed the switch that put out all the lamps as he left the drawing room. Turning his mind to the practicalities of the situation, he vowed to speak to Miriam first thing in the morning about preparing for the newest member of their household.

The Saturday at the end of the month was the date they had agreed that Ellie would move into the Park Lane house, and if by then she had not found someone to rent or buy her own property then Nikolai would step in and find a suitable agency to do so for her. And just as soon as a civil marriage could be arranged between them at the local register office their union would be sanctioned officially. Life would continue on more or less as normal…the only difference being that now he would have a wife and Arina a mother…

Ellie put her arm round the thin, hunched figure seated on the threadbare couch beside her. 'Jay?' she said gently, aware that the boy was crying and didn't want her to see. 'Tell me what happened.'

Scrubbing at his tears with his tobacco-stained nail-bitten fingers, he turned his resentful and hurt gaze towards her. 'I saw her… I saw me mum with her new bloke in the high street. She acted like she didn't even know who I was! I was staring at her and she looked right through me!'

'What did you say to her?'

'Nothin'!' His expression was savage. 'What was the point? She'd probably just ignore me anyway! You could see she was more interested in the loser by her side! All loved up, she was, and happy…happy that she wasn't with *me*!'

'Do you know where she's staying?'

'No—and I don't want to either!'

'It must have been hard for you…'

Absently stroking the boy's straight dark hair, Ellie soothed him as though he were a child. It didn't matter what the textbooks or the rules said—in her opinion when someone was hurting they needed the warmth and reassurance of human contact and Jay had been fending for himself since he was a small boy. His alcohol-addicted mother had inflicted a series of woefully inadequate and violent men on her son in her desperate search for a relationship.

'Seeing her again must have opened up old wounds. But you're getting your life together without her, Jay,' she reminded him. 'Next Saturday you're moving out of the shelter into a room of your own, and on Monday you're starting your apprenticeship at the timber merchants. Things are moving on for you too. Soon you'll be earning your first real wage packet, and life is just going to get better and better!'

The teenager sniffed and looked her straight in the eyes. 'It'll be great moving out of here! Not that it ain't any good, but it ain't exactly a palace is it?'

His dark gaze wryly swept the uncurtained barely furnished room, with its tatty cushions on the floor, the single couch, and the fireplace with its inadequate electric bar heater. It tenderly moved Ellie that a lad who had never had much more than this scruffy room in the whole of his life should nurture aspirations for something better.

'It'll be so cool, having me own place! You've been a real friend to me, miss… I couldn't have got through the last six months without you. The things you said… always so positive and upbeat…well, it gave me something to hang onto.'

Slowly moving her hand from his hair onto her lap, Ellie smiled. It touched her more than she could say to have someone like Jay affirm that she'd been a help to him, and she was reminded yet again why she kept on doing her work at the shelter even when she had a counselling practice of her own to run.

'It was my pleasure. I know it's been tough for you, but just try and take one day at a time, hmm? Use some of the relaxation skills I taught you when life gets overwhelming, and remember that you can always stay in touch if you need someone to talk to. Everyone here is rooting for you too…don't forget that.'

'I won't, miss…and thanks again.'

It wasn't only Jay who was moving to a new abode on Saturday. The two weeks had flown by since she and Nikolai had made their agreement. One of her colleagues at the centre had agreed to rent her flat indefinitely, and the realisation that it was now payback time swept disturbingly through Ellie again and again—at work, and mercilessly in the evenings, when she was back home.

Carrying her mug of instant coffee from the kitchen into the living room that particular night, it hit her even more forcefully just what she had agreed to with Nikolai. *She was doing it for Arina*, she told herself, blanking out the flickering images on the muted television screen in front of her in order to think. *And for her father...* There was no way she would run the risk of him going to prison again, should she decline the marriage and Nikolai bring a private case against them—even if his suspicions that she had stolen from him were completely unfounded.

On the phone to her earlier from Edinburgh, her dad had told her how bad things were getting with his health and Ellie's stomach had churned with anxiety and sorrow. Nikolai Golitsyn might do anything and everything he could to ensure his daughter's happiness, but he was also possessed of a mercenary streak that she would no doubt become all too aware of should Ellie disappoint him in his ambition to make her his wife. There was simply no talking him out of this idea of his.

Every day on the phone when he rang her at work, he reminded her of that. His mind was made up. And never far from Ellie's thoughts about the new life she had in store was the heart-racing notion of sleeping with Nikolai. She hadn't put up a fight about that because part of her hoped that if there was intimacy between them there might eventually be trust, and...and something more perhaps. Ellie wouldn't even say the word in private to herself, it seemed so impossible. The fact was—blackmailer or not—he was the man she had *always* secretly desired. But from Hackney to Park Lane! It was a surreal prospect.

Leaving her coffee on a small side table, she dropped down onto the comfy striped couch and shook her head in apprehension and wonder. Ellie wondered what her colleagues and the volunteers at the shelter would make of the dramatic improvement in the location where she lived. And there would be the stress and inconvenience of her longer journey to work everyday. It was hard to feel excitement or pleasure in the upcoming move—apart from the joy of being with Arina at last. How *could* she anticipate it with any sense of contentment or satisfaction when underlying it all was the genuinely gut-wrenching prospect of living in the one place from her past that had caused her more sorrow and regret than any part of her emotionally impoverished upbringing as a child?

'Is that all of your bags, Dr Lyons?' Nikolai's housekeeper met Ellie at the front door and invited her into the hall.

'My other stuff is arriving later… Nikolai—I mean Mr Golitsyn has arranged it for me.'

'Well, then, I will take you upstairs and show you to your room!'

'By the way…where *is* Mr Golitsyn? Isn't he here?'

'No, Dr Lyons. He has taken the little one to her ballet lesson. He said to tell you that he will join you later and to please make yourself at home.'

'I see.'

An unexpected reprieve then…

Ellie breathed an inward sigh of relief when the

housekeeper led her away from the room she had occupied five years ago. That had been beautifully appointed and decorated, but being there she knew she would have been catapulted all too swiftly into the past again, and would have felt herself at a disadvantage somehow, when she needed to garner all the positives she could muster. Determination was strengthening inside her that, for however long this strange arrangement with Nikolai lasted, she would make a decent go of it...for Arina's sake if nothing else. And, yes, she would let him see that she was a very different woman today from the inexperienced and perhaps naïve girl she'd been when she had worked for him before. He might have blackmailed her into this unwanted partnership by using Arina as a bargaining tool, but he wouldn't have everything his own way! Not by a long chalk!

Following the plump housekeeper down a corridor on the topmost floor, Ellie felt her heartbeat accelerate as another troubling thought speared her. What if she was being led to Nikolai's bedroom? She'd agreed that they would be intimate once they were married, but she'd hoped he wouldn't take that to mean as soon as she moved in. She needed time to adjust.

But, no... This exquisitely light and airy, room with its scented air, elegant armoire, and a double bed with a rich Venetian purple silk bedspread was, Miriam announced with a smile, 'one of my favourite guest rooms.' It even had a lovely balcony that looked out onto the garden.

Alone again, with Miriam's cheerful promise of a cup of tea and a slice of home-made fruitcake when she returned downstairs ringing enticingly in her ears, Ellie left her bags where they were and went and sat down on the bed. Smoothing her hand over the sumptuous silk counterpane with a softly weary sigh, she felt as though extreme fatigue—both emotional and physical—had finally caught up with her. She'd worked at the shelter nearly every night this week, after working all day at the practice, and it was no wonder her body was practically screaming at her to rest!

If Nikolai and Arina were going to be a while, would it matter if she stole ten minutes or so and had a nap? Unable to resist doing just that, Ellie kicked off the narrow-heeled pumps that had been pinching her toes all morning, and scooted up the bed to rest her head against the luxurious pillows. With another grateful sigh that seemed to arise from the very depths of her soul, she shut her eyes—and in less than a minute had drifted off into a deep, deep slumber…

'Ellie?' Nikolai knocked on the door for a second time. Miriam had assured him that Dr Lyons had not come down from her room since she had shown her there, and that had been over an hour ago. Leaving a hungry and happy Arina eating fruitcake in the kitchen with the older woman, Nikolai had come upstairs to see for himself what was keeping Ellie.

He had not set eyes on her for over two weeks now, and he could not deny that a quiet but fierce excitement was building inside him to redress that. When he received no response from her yet again, he turned the doorknob and stepped inside. A shaft of buttery golden sunlight streamed through the old-fashioned window, casting a dappled effect on the carpet that showed the shadow of trembling leaves from the oak tree in the garden. But it wasn't that captivating sight that drew Nikolai's attention.

Ellie was lying on the bed, fast asleep. The quietly hypnotic rhythm of her breathing was the only sound in the room. He moved nearer to the bed, all his muscles helplessly contracting at the vision of her lovely face, golden hair, and her sweetly curvaceous body clothed in black jeans and a lilac coloured sweater. He found himself smiling at the sight of her small slender feet with their rose-pink-painted toenails curled into the silk counterpane, and suddenly he was in no great hurry to return to the kitchen.

If Nikolai didn't confess at least to himself that he had feared Ellie might find some way of not keeping the bargain they had made he would be a liar. And now that he had the very real and captivating evidence of her presence before him something inside him knew a great longing to keep her to himself for as long as possible before resuming the rest of his day.

Stirring a little in her sleep, Ellie had a sudden furrow between her smooth arched brows. 'Sasha—no!'

The heartfelt whimper left her lips and Nikolai's muscles clenched again, this time in shock and dismay and…yes…slow-burning rage too. There he stood, admiring her beauty like the most gullible fool on the planet, relieved that she had not reneged on their agreement and grasping at the slimmest hope that things might turn out for the best after all—and Ellie betrayed him yet again… Betrayed him with a dream of his brother Sasha!

Disturbed by the images that flitted across the inner landscape of her mind, Ellie opened her stunning emerald eyes and stared at Nikolai in shock, instantly alert. 'What's wrong? What are you doing here?' She pushed herself up into a sitting position, her not quite steady hand smoothing back the lock of bright hair that had flopped onto her forehead.

'Nothing is wrong. I merely came up to see where you were. Miriam said she brought you up here over an hour ago.'

'I fell asleep.'

'Obviously…'

Crossing his arms over his chest, Nikolai speared her with an accusing and blaming glance. 'You were dreaming about Sasha.'

'Was I?'

'You called out his name.'

'Did I? I don't remember.' Swinging her legs over the side of the bed, Ellie let her bare feet touch the floor. Swaying slightly, she stood, momentarily losing her balance.

Nikolai automatically moved forward to help steady her, his hands settling on either side of her rounded hips. He let them stay there as his furious gaze duelled with hers. He was entrapped by the enticing warmth that flowed into his palms and suddenly—shockingly— he craved a far more *intimate* contact…

'You seem to have an ongoing problem with your memory, Ellie. Can you blame me if I am beginning to believe it is a selective loss?'

'Believe what you like!' Resentfully, she freed

herself and moved as far away from him as she could. 'The only reason I'm here is because of Arina and my father. I guess I'll just have to learn to live with your less than flattering opinions of me!'

Nikolai shrugged, suddenly lazily amused by her show of spirit and—despite his anger over her dream— still aroused too. 'So be it. How do you like your room, by the way?'

He saw her indignation deflate. The slender shoulders in the lilac sweater lifted in a shrug. 'It's very nice. Pretty. I like the view over the garden.'

'Good. Once we are married you will move into my room. It too has a nice view over the garden.'

Smiling enigmatically, Nikolai had the satisfaction of seeing Ellie's expressive eyes widen. If Sasha had enjoyed the comfort and pleasure of her seductive body then why shouldn't he? There was no reason for Nikolai to feel any guilt whatsoever. After all, in a very short time she would legitimately be his wife.

'You still look a little tired. What have you been doing, Ellie? Burning the candle at both ends? Partying, perhaps, with the new celebrity friends you have made at the television studios?'

'You're determined only to think the very worst of me, aren't you?' She shook her head a little forlornly.

'I see what appears to be right in front of my eyes!'

'Then that's your first mistake! Do you make all your judgements with so little hard evidence to back them up?'

Feeling strangely chastised, Nikolai impatiently brushed off Ellie's unsettling remark and moved towards the door. 'It's time we went downstairs. Miriam has made some tea for us, and Arina is waiting to see you also.'

'Talking of Arina—what have you told her about me? I mean…why I'm staying here?'

'I explained to her a little while ago that you were her mother's sister—her aunt. I told her that when we recently met up again I was thinking about how you used to take care of her as a baby and how close you were to her. Nearly every other day she asks me… "When will I have a mother?" So I told her that I had decided you were the perfect person for the job, and that when I asked you, you said you would happily accept.'

'Children always sense a lie.'

Refusing to let her comment rattle him, Nikolai lifted his broad shoulders in their trademark shrug—a gesture he often employed to disguise his true feelings. In business particularly it didn't pay to let the opposition know what you were thinking. 'I will do whatever I have to do to make her happy! I already told you that. If you try and tell her anything different about why you are here, then I will see to it that you regret it to the end of your days!'

'Any more threats?' Ellie raised her chin defiantly.

Unable to stop the smile that tugged at the edges of his mouth, Nikolai shook his head. 'For now, Ellie… I am all out of threats. What I would like to happen is for you to come downstairs and drink tea with my daughter and me! Not too difficult a task even for you…do you agree?'

'And what about your friends? What will you tell *them* about me?' she persisted.

'I will tell them the truth. That you are Arina's aunt and my fiancée…and that we are soon to be married.' Without giving her a chance to comment, Nikolai abruptly left the room—not even glancing over his shoulder to see if she would join him…

The items Ellie had left behind her in the flat—the things she couldn't do without, like her wardrobe of clothes, her compact music system, CD collection and two bookcases of books—arrived soon after she'd finished drinking tea with Nikolai, sampling Miriam's knockout fruitcake and playing for a while with an excited Arina.

The little girl had kept giving Ellie long, assessing happy glances when she'd thought she wasn't looking, and that had made her heart squeeze. The child was very easy to love. That much was starkly and worryingly evident. And Ellie knew that the more she allowed herself to build up a relationship with Nikolai's enchanting daughter—*her niece*—the harder it would be when this pretend union of theirs failed—as fail it inevitably would. And yet again Arina would be the sad casualty of that failure in a tragic story that seemed impossible to resolve.

Now, in the lovely room she had been allocated to sleep in, Ellie tried to put aside all thoughts of the future and concentrate on the present instead. The removal men who had transported her things had positioned her two pine bookcases side by side against one of the professionally painted lavender walls, and now she got down on her knees and started to excavate the six packed cardboard boxes of books they had brought too. Briefly she wondered how Jay was getting on with *his* move today.

Glancing round the genteel bedroom, with its expensive handcrafted furniture and the open balcony doors that let in the sound of birdsong and the scent of late-blooming roses from the garden, she felt her stomach momentarily turn over. The contrast in their new abodes was poignantly painful. Yet for all the room's beauty Ellie wasn't totally happy to be there at all. If it weren't for Arina—and the threat that hung over her that she might not ever see her again if Ellie reneged on the agreement she'd made with Nikolai—she would be more than content to be back in her flat in Hackney, with the constant flow of noisy traffic streaming past her door and the smell of curry wafting through the opened windows from the Bangladeshi restaurant at the end of the street.

Sighing, she turned her attention back to the task in hand. She was turning the page of a favourite hardback she'd revisited time and time again, unable to resist casting her eager gaze over the opening chapter, when her mind was seized by the memory of the dream that had earlier disturbed her nap. She'd *lied* when she'd insisted to Nikolai that she hadn't remembered dreaming about Sasha, and now the painfully real scene frighteningly replayed itself.

They were standing downstairs at the front door, and Sasha had the baby in his arms. Arina was crying loudly in distress, obviously sensing something wasn't right, and Ellie was begging him to give the baby back to her. For answer, Sasha gave her a disturbing and confused smile. He was high on drugs again, Ellie realised, as well as drunk, and he was demanding that Ellie drive him to see a friend of his—a 'friend' that she somehow knew supplied him with drugs. His habit had worsened since her sister had died, and Ellie had often pleaded with him to give it up—if not for his own sake than at least for his child's. He always promised he would, but Ellie had long known he was finding it impossible to keep that promise.

Many times she'd threatened to tell Nikolai just what was happening, but more often than not Sasha would start pleading with her to give him 'one more chance'—and she would again keep quiet about the problem. But as he'd stood swaying at the front door in the dream—beyond reason and maybe beyond hope—Ellie fervently wished she had confided in Nikolai about what was going on with his brother. 'Please, Ellie—take me to my friend's. Or I swear I will disappear for good, and Arina and Nikolai will never see me again!' Sasha begged, glassy-eyed.

'You know I can't drive you, Sasha! I've only just passed my test, and I don't even have my own car yet!' Ellie replied, her heart thumping with foreboding and dread.

'You can drive my brother's car.'

'You're joking!'

'Then I'll phone for a cab.'

That was not a good idea… What if the cab driver went to the newspapers and exposed Sasha's drug problem to the world? His brother was both well known and respected, and had surely been through enough trauma without being dragged into the seedy orbit of a voracious and unkind media! It felt as if Ellie was in the worst dilemma of her life.

A second later there was a sound in her mind like a heavy door slamming shut, and it echoed for long seconds even as the rest of the dream frustratingly evaded her. *Was it dream or memory*? Hardly realising she was holding her breath, Ellie let out the trapped air in her lungs with a sound like a woman in labour. Into the stillness that followed came a knock at the door.

'Yes?'

She prayed it wouldn't be Nikolai. The memory of the dream clung to her like the cold slimy reeds found growing in marshes, and she didn't think she'd be able to keep her distress or her guilt hidden. But her visitor was Miriam.

'I am very sorry to trouble you, Dr Lyons—but Mr Golitsyn, he is going out very shortly and would like you to accompany him.'

'Where to?'

A fond, doting look crept over the housekeeper's face. 'To take the little one shopping for clothes! He said to tell you he would value your opinion.'

Her disturbing dream put firmly aside, Ellie rose slowly to her feet and dusted down her jeans. An undeniable sense of surprise and pleasure had inexplicably swept through her at the idea that Nikolai had thought to ask her to go with them.

'Tell him I'll be down in about ten minutes.' She smiled, inwardly assuring herself the pleasure she had experienced had been at the prospect of spending time with Arina.

'I will tell him, Dr Lyons.'

'Oh—and Miriam? Why don't you just call me Ellie?'

CHAPTER SEVEN

THEY'D VISITED ALL the major department stores in the west end to source suitable clothing for a six-year-old, and afterwards—as if he hadn't already spent a small fortune—Nikolai had told his driver to take them to the King's Road in Chelsea.

It was clear that Arina was absolutely *loving* her shopping spree! She was a real 'girly girl', scorning jeans and more unisex clothing in favour of extremely feminine and pretty dresses, with shoes and accessories to match! And the child wasn't the only one who appeared to be in her element. Nikolai was more relaxed and at ease than Ellie had ever seen him, and definitely in an indulgent mood. Dressed in a sky-blue polo shirt and dark jeans, with a casual tan-coloured suede jacket, he looked like any other well-dressed professional enjoying an outing with his family.

Family… The word was like a pool full of sharks as far as Ellie was concerned. Part of her was torn, wanting to be the mother that Arina clearly craved and needed, and yet she was completely daunted by the very idea.

She hadn't even known her own mother, as she had died shortly after giving birth to Ellie, so what examples of motherhood could she draw upon when she had more or less brought herself up? And she was even more troubled by the idea of letting her guard slip even an inch around Arina's father. Would he or *could* he ever see past his need to make her pay for what had happened in the past and discover the real woman behind the imagined misdeeds? It was hard to believe such a thing could happen.

Whatever way Ellie viewed it, he had coerced her into making this deal with him, he didn't trust her, thought her a liar and a thief, and—worst of all—believed her to have been having an affair with his brother! The thought slammed into her like a freight train, stealing her joy at admiring yet another pretty outfit that she had helped Arina try on in the small exclusive boutique.

'Ellie?' Nikolai's hypnotic voice invaded her consciousness, and she glanced up at him in surprise across the too-warm room with its select display of colourful clothing, immediately magnetised by it.

'You were miles away.'

'Sorry,' she mumbled, fixing a smile on her face and crouching down to buckle the red patent leather shoes that went with Arina's outfit.

Outside again in the sunshine, Nikolai firmly clasped his daughter's hand, and touched Ellie's arm when she would have walked on.

'You now have a choice,' he announced seriously. 'We can either go clothes-shopping for you, or pay a visit to the Russian tearooms that have recently opened up nearby.'

'I really don't need new clothes!' she answered sharply, almost faint with embarrassment at the idea he would buy *anything* for her…let alone something as personal as clothing! But in the Russian's unsettling and riveting glance was distinct evidence of humour.

His gaze swept over Ellie's fitted black jeans, and the scooped-neck white T-shirt that hugged her breasts a little too snugly, as if he was thinking her dress sense certainly needed improving upon even if she didn't think it did! There was something else in that not so innocent glance that made Ellie break out in an almost excruciatingly hot sweat beneath her clothes as she devastatingly remembered the way Nikolai had clasped her hips when he had stopped her from stumbling in the bedroom earlier. *As if all he had needed was her consent and he would have brought them right up against his own…*

'It is an unusual woman, in my experience, who denies she needs anything when the opportunity to be taken shopping is offered to her!' he remarked in that measured, sensual way he had of speaking sometimes— a way that was almost too mesmerising for words.

'Well, I've never exactly been a huge fan of shopping.' Glancing wryly down at the shiny designer carrier bags that were packed full of Arina's new clothes, Ellie hoped Nikolai wouldn't think she was simply pretending not to be interested. *It was a miserable feeling to be with someone who didn't believe you were capable of being honest.* A deep, underlying impulse arose inside her for him to see that she was both truthful and had integrity. 'I'd rather spend my free time reading a good book or going for a walk! Not that I haven't enjoyed helping Arina choose her new clothes…that's something entirely different. It's been the most fun I've had in ages!'

'I love my new shiny red shoes!' The child beamed up at her. 'Did you have shiny red shoes when you were a little girl like me, Ellie?'

The innocent question made Ellie's throat tighten briefly with anguish. When she was small all her clothing and shoes had been one hundred per cent charity donations. Except for a blue and white checked dress one of her kinder foster-carers had bought her for her seventh birthday. To this day Ellie recalled the freshly starched shop-bought smell of it with a mixture of happiness and childish hurt that it had not been her father who had bought it for her.

'No darling… I didn't.'

'So that is settled, then. We will go to the Russian tearooms!' As if sensing she had had a difficult moment replying to his daughter's question, Nikolai assumed his usual authoritative stance and stepped in to deflect any more painful enquiries. 'But first let us take these very heavy bags back to the car, before my arms either get stretched beyond repair or drop off!'

'Silly Papa!' Arina grinned up at him in delight.

The interior of the new tearooms was almost as ornate as any Russian orthodox church, with its lavish gold and black décor, and row upon row of seats uphol-stered in deep crimson velvet—just like pews. Between them were stout, sturdy-legged mahogany tables, and on top of them candles enclosed in intricately patterned gold lanterns.

It reminded Nikolai of many of the grandly imposing interiors of buildings he recalled from his time as a child in Moscow—clearly no expense had been spared in creating something close to authenticity. It looked as if business was going well too. Nearly every table was full.

It so happened that Nikolai was acquainted with the proprietor. In the business community in London people from the same country often tended to meet and socialise as a matter of course. And the short, stout man behind the counter, with wiry grey hair and half-moon glasses practically leapt out of his seat when he saw Nikolai and the two girls come in. No mean feat when one took into account his generous girth.

'Nikolai!'

There followed a welcome in Russian that would have pleased the old Tsar himself, Nikolai thought in secret amusement.

'Let me show you and your guests to my very best table—I reserve it for VIPs!' Beaming at Ellie and Arina, the man's face was almost florid with excitement at having the opportunity to welcome a man of Nikolai's standing into his establishment.

Nikolai knew that word would very quickly go round with all the details of his visit.

'Is this your family?' the older man enquired as they seated themselves at a table that had the best vantage point in the place—up a small flight of wide steps, with a clear view of everyone who came in the door, yet with its sensuous scarlet drapes almost enclosing them, providing a sense of privacy as well.

'Yes,' Nikolai answered in English, sensing the slight discomfort on Ellie's revealing face at the barrier of language that excluded her from the conversation. 'This is my daughter Arina and my fiancée Elizabeth.'

He uttered the words confidently, without hesitation, and immediately observed the soft rose-pink colour that invaded Ellie's cheeks. For a briefly electric moment Nikolai's gaze met hers and held it. She had the most magnetically beautiful eyes he had ever seen in a woman, and he fell into a kind of trance. It was no wonder Sasha had not been able to resist her. The thought was hardly a welcome one, and rubbed salt into wounds that were still smarting. Bitterness flowed into the pit of his stomach. If Sasha had lived, would she still be with him now? Living on the proceeds of his mother's diamond necklace?

'I am honoured to meet your lovely fiancée and your beautiful daughter!' the tearooms' proprietor declared, including them all in the effusive beam of his smile. 'Now, shall I leave you with the menu, or do you already know what you would like?'

'We have only come in for dessert and some tea,' Nikolai replied, delving deep inside himself to restore his threatened equilibrium. 'Some blinis, perhaps? With honey or—'

'Chocolate sauce!' Arina interrupted excitedly, her dark eyes shining. 'Ellie, you must have blinis with chocolate sauce! They're my favourite!'

'Blinis?' She glanced quizzically at the child, and

then at her father, her heart racing a little because of that look he had exchanged with her just a moment ago. A look that had made her insides soften and melt like marshmallows being held over a flame…

'Pancakes,' he explained.

'Oh…'

'So… We will have a selection of cream, chocolate sauce and fruit with some blinis and some tea, I think. Ellie…are you happy with tea, or would you prefer coffee?'

'Tea is fine, thanks.'

'Arina? Would you like a banana milkshake? I know that is your favourite too.'

'Yes, please, Papa!'

Briefly inclining his head in thanks, Nikolai waited until the owner had left the table before speaking again. Resting his elbows on the table and linking his hands, he told himself he was firmly back in control again, and would try not to let unpleasant and corrosive thoughts of Ellie and his brother together spoil this outing he had wanted them to enjoy together as a family.

'I never asked you before…' Ellie began, touching the tips of her fingers to a stray wheat-blonde curl. 'Did you grow up in Russia?'

'In Moscow—yes.'

'What was it like?'

The genuine interest in her voice took him aback. 'For me and my family?' Nikolai reflected for a moment on the past, and the culture that had helped shape him. 'We were fortunate in having a very good life compared to many. My father was a scientist—a member of the intelligentsia… He became an entrepreneur when oil was discovered on our land. He provided for my brother and me all the things that anyone could wish for their children, and we were able to experience many enjoyable things…including travel. Something that was not available to everyone, I am afraid…'

'I hear it's a very beautiful city.'

'It is. Although in recent years it has undergone many, many changes. And there are over two hundred nationalities in the country that have the challenge of getting along!'

'Relationships are definitely the biggest challenge for all of us.' Looking thoughtful, then embarrassed, as though realising she'd inadvertently introduced a topic that she would prefer to steer clear of in light of the circumstances, Ellie turned to her niece, sitting beside her. 'So, how did you enjoy your ballet class this morning?' she asked.

'It was good!'

'Perhaps next time I can come and watch you?'

'Yes, I would like that. You can come and watch with Papa!'

'And when we get home today I'll help you put all your lovely new things away, but perhaps you can try them all on again first, and we can have a little fashion parade?'

'Oh, yes, please!'

Witnessing the sheer joy on his little girl's face at Ellie's suggestions, and the way her dark gaze watched the lovely woman by her side with a possessiveness and pride that made his heart turn over, Nikolai was gratefully reminded of all the qualities that he admired in Ellie. She was a natural with children. He had seen that from the start and had never forgotten it. She also had a great tenderness in her that she did not hesitate to display when she was around them. Blackmail or no, he had definitely done the right thing in choosing her as Arina's new mother. Whatever happened between them she would not disappoint his child, he was certain…

'And what about you, Ellie?' he asked, his pulse helplessly speeding up as she turned her arresting emerald gaze back to him. 'What about your own childhood? Did you always live in London?'

'Yes.' There was definite hesitation in both her eyes and her voice, and Nikolai frowned as annoyance replaced his previous magnanimity towards her. *Why did she always seem to be hiding something from him*?

'What part of London?' he probed.

'All over.' She lifted her slender shoulders in a defensive shrug. 'I moved around a lot.'

'Why did your parents not settle somewhere?'

'My mother died before I was a year old, and my father—my father wasn't around a lot of the time.'

'Why not?' *Because he was spending time in prison*? Nikolai speculated. If so, what had happened to Ellie and Jackie when he was away?

'He didn't live with me and my sister for a long time. We spent most of our childhood and early teenage years in either foster-homes or children's homes. Not always together, either.' Her pretty mouth tightened, and even Arina became still with attention.

'Your father did not want to raise you both?' Now Nikolai was feeling something very different from annoyance and suspicion.

Lifting the water jug a passing waitress had brought to their table, Ellie poured herself a glass and sipped at it carefully before replying. 'I don't think this is something we should discuss in front of Arina. Can we leave it for another time, do you think?'

CHAPTER EIGHT

ELLIE was drawing a bath when there was a knock at the door. Cursing softly, she turned off the taps. Raising her arms to stretch out the kinks in her back, she realised the day had taken far more out of her than she'd estimated it would. Her first day as a member of the Golitsyn family—moving in, going shopping, eating blinis with chocolate sauce at the Russian tearooms, followed later by a family dinner prepared and cooked by the housekeeper. It would not normally make a body so tired, she was certain. But trying to control her emotions, always too close to the surface, and retain her composure when she seemed to be constantly under Nikolai's intimidating scrutiny had drained her right down to the marrow.

It simply wasn't possible to have any kind of conversation or contact with her formidable husband-to-be without fearing she was digging herself into an even bigger hole than she was in already. Regularly Ellie found herself wondering what other skeletons he would convince himself he'd found in her closet to trap her with.

'You are getting ready for bed?'

Her eyes nearly popped out of her head when she found the subject of her nervous musing on the other side of the door. It was an innocent enough question, seeing as she was standing there dressed only in a light cotton wrap, but the way Nikolai's eyes tracked slowly and deliberately down her body made it seem much more provocative.

'I was just running a bath before I turned in…yes,' she answered, wishing her voice didn't sound so strained and anxious.

'There is something I wanted to ask you, and with Arina present at dinner I did not get the chance. Can I come in?'

Not seeing how she could possibly refuse him, Ellie reluctantly stepped to the side. The boxes full of books she'd planned to sort earlier remained mostly unopened on the carpet, and various pieces of clothing she had attempted to arrange into some kind of order before hanging them in the wardrobe or folding them onto the scented shelves in the armoire were scattered in a riot of colour over the sumptuous silk bedspread. Seeing Nikolai glance towards the various piles, and noticing that the one in the foremost position in his eyeline was a little stack of lacy underwear she had folded, Ellie felt her limbs suddenly become as fluid as water.

'What is it that you wanted to ask me?' Her fingers fumbled with the loosely tied knot in the belt of her robe, and she prayed it was more secure than it felt.

'The same question that I asked you in the tearooms.' He took a couple of steps towards her, then came to a standstill, dropping his hands casually either side of the straight lean hips encased in softly napped denim. A frown appeared between his dark blond brows. 'Why was it that your father did not raise you and Jackie, Ellie? I would like to know.'

Not knowing why it could possibly matter to him, Ellie sighed heavily. Psychologist or not, she was always fairly reluctant to revisit her own past—preferring to concentrate on the present as much as she possibly could. She frequently schooled her clients that they were much more than their personal histories or stories— that life could be created afresh at any chosen moment…

'When my mother died, for a long time my father blamed me for her death. She was weak after my birth, and a chest infection turned into pneumonia. He loved her so much, and couldn't get over it when he lost her. He struggled with being a single parent and then he decided he couldn't look after me and Jackie any longer. So he contacted Social Services to look for a foster-home for us both. They found me somewhere straight away, but Jackie—who was a couple of years older— was installed in a children's home. I was about three when I went to a new set of foster-carers—a young couple who had been trying for a baby for a couple of years without success. A year later they did have a baby of their own, and decided an active four-year-old was too difficult to manage as well, so I too was installed in the children's home. I spent the next few years until I was sixteen going from foster-carer to foster-carer, and sometimes back to the home. A large chunk of that time Jackie and I spent apart. Does that answer your question?'

'So when did your father come back on the scene?'

'Just before my sixteenth birthday. He'd kept in touch with Social Services, and from time to time sent money for me and Jackie. Over the years I think he really regretted giving us up. He had a change of heart, you see. He'd had a couple of failed relationships, and no doubt saw a lonely old age staring him in the face if he didn't make contact with his family again.'

Ellie's smile was thin, she knew…perhaps not quite as convincing as she wanted it to be to show Nikolai that it was all ancient history, and she was shocked by the hurt she heard in her own tone—a hurt she really thought she'd dealt with and long buried. *Especially since her father had become ill.* Ellie could only conclude that the anxieties of the day had undermined her.

'And you forgave him? Just like that?'

'Yes.' It hadn't been easy. There had been times when Ellie had wanted to punish her father for his desertion—as he had punished her and her sister—and cut him off for ever. But she just hadn't been able to bring herself to do it. Not when he had literally *begged* her to give him another chance. Besides…hadn't they both endured enough heartache and pain?

'I can't believe I did not know this. Jackie and you never really spoke of your past, but that was a tough beginning you had…by anyone's standards.'

'Maybe so.' She shrugged. 'I certainly learned some valuable lessons about how to survive. Jackie didn't like to look back, but it's helped me in many ways. It's helped me realise that I want to help others who've had similar experiences to me. Anyway…nobody escapes life's challenges—no matter what their upbringing or circumstances.'

For a moment or two Nikolai seemed to be considering that, then he folded his arms over his chest and sighed.

'In the light of what you have just explained I think I can understand why you were tempted to have an affair with Sasha. The promise of an easier time instead of perpetual struggle must have seemed very appealing. Not that I am about to condone the affair…or the stealing of the necklace!'

After being inadvertently led to reveal some of the pain behind her upbringing, Ellie felt Nikolai's cynical assumption of her having an affair with his brother as well as being complicit in the theft of a valuable necklace like a kick in the teeth. Once again she was sick with misery. Silently she cursed the memory that eluded her, which she was certain would attest to her innocence.

'Well, I've told you what you wanted to know. I'd like to take my bath now and then go to bed. It's been a long day.'

Weary of conflict, all Ellie wanted now was for Nikolai to leave her alone and let her be for a while. But he didn't do that. Instead he moved even closer to her, and shockingly placed his hands on her upper arms.

'You would not have had an easier time with my brother. That is the truth. He would only have added to your heartache.'

His words took Ellie aback even more than the touch that burned like flame through the flimsy cotton of her wrap. She had never heard Nikolai speak ill of Sasha before, even when it had become obvious to all the members of the Golitsyn household that the younger man had driven him to distraction with his constant demands for money, his irresponsible, lackadaisical attitude and his complete lack of concern for his baby daughter.

'What makes you so sure I wanted to be with him in the first place?'

Ellie was trembling as she asked the question, because Nikolai's hands seemed to firm against her arms rather than withdraw. Up close, he had a clean fresh smell that reminded her of newly laundered clothing spritzed with lemon. But underlying that evocative scent were darker more earthier tones, suggestive of elements much more disturbing to the senses.

Why couldn't she seem to move all of a sudden? It was almost as if she didn't *want* to be free of his touch, or the sizzling cerulean gaze that seared her soul and shook her violently awake. More awake than she had been in years...

'Perhaps you were lonely, Ellie?' His tone was husky, and suddenly the pad of his thumb was following the soft vulnerable curve of her tender lower lip, pressing her flesh with provocative intent, and wisps of his not quite steady breath were skimming over her skin like the lightest strokes from a feather.

'Loneliness would never have driven me into his arms...or made me steal for him!' Her eyes swam with tears. She had been beyond lonely for so long—but nothing, she was sure, would have made her want to try and soothe that forlorn ache with a man as unstable as Sasha. However charming he had sometimes been.

'And what about *my* arms, Ellie?'

'What?'

'Have you forgotten the evening before the accident as well?'

In shock, Ellie met Nikolai's brooding steady gaze. The scene that for the past five years she had striven hard to keep at bay played out again in her mind. What good would it have done her to recall such things when all had ended in pain and disaster? But what had transpired between them returned to her now, in a rich, full-blooded tapestry of spine-tingling memory. *Nikolai had kissed her.* Yes, kissed her as though his life depended on it. His erotically velvet mouth had plundered hers with passionately hungry demand, and Ellie had been swept away by the urgent sexual hunger that had deluged her too. His heat and hardness had burned through her clothing wherever he had touched her, and she had responded like a woman starving for breath as shock-waves of lust and rapture never before imagined or experienced had assailed her.

The only thing that had prevented the inevitable heart-pounding, pulse-racing outcome of that hot wild embrace had been the disturbing sudden peal of the telephone on Nikolai's desk. Like a scythe cutting through their stunned senses, it had brought them violently back down to earth and Ellie had fled to her room—stunned to the core by the realisation that she had been about to surrender herself to the powerful, charismatic *married* man she worked for without so much as a thought to the consequences.

With satisfaction Nikolai saw that Ellie did indeed

remember what had happened between them that night. The longing and desire that had been inexorably building in his blood ever since she had opened the door and allowed him into her room increased with stunning force. Exhaling softly, he moved the pad of his thumb from her bewitchingly full lower lip to trace her fine-boned jawline, until finally he cupped it in his hand. Pleasure and need drowned him. The extremely erotic scent she exuded, and the warmth from her soft, sweetly curvaceous body had him all but hypnotised. And it only added to the agony of pleasure inside him when he hazarded a guess that underneath her insubstantial robe she was naked.

For a long moment Nikolai's will was locked in a battle for supremacy over his desire. Primal instinct vied with a logic he really did not want to entertain, and logic was losing fast. The living, breathing reality of this woman was simply too much temptation for one mortal man.

'I'm not looking for a cure for loneliness!' Her mouth working to contain her distress, Ellie stepped abruptly away from Nikolai and put herself firmly out of his reach. Suddenly the decision to take things further was no longer his. Her lush green eyes glowed like malachite in the lamplit room. 'And if I was, it certainly wouldn't be with you!'

'But you *will* share my bed when we are married, Ellie! We have an agreement, remember? Do not imagine for one moment that I have changed my mind about that part of it, because I fully intend to hold you to your word!'

'You don't have to worry that I won't keep my

promise, but it won't happen until we are married…and then only under duress!'

A throaty chuckle escaped Nikolai's lips. Maybe it was arrogant of him, but he already knew that the heat between them that had erupted in that never-to-be-forgotten evening before the accident was easily going to flare up again, and would undoubtedly conclude with Ellie being in his arms and in his bed before much more time elapsed. To try and deny the kind of combustible chemistry they had would be as impossible as trying to stop a raging river from flowing downstream. No matter how much will-power or determination you applied to the task, in the end the outcome was inevitable.

'You may fool yourself that it will be under duress when you finally share my bed, Ellie… But I know you are not immune to my touch, and clearly you have needs just as I have needs. Do not trouble to try and deny it!'

'So that gives you the right to just *demand* that I sleep with you? Listen… I may have had no choice but to make this arrangement with you, but that doesn't mean that you *own* me! Why don't you just forget about the idea of sleeping with me and find some other more willing woman to accommodate you in that area?'

'Like a mistress, you mean?' Both irked and amused, Nikolai slowly shook his head. 'Why should I bother with a mistress when I will have a beautiful wife to keep me warm at night? Besides, I want to set a good example for my daughter. I want nothing to make her doubt that her father and mother are absolutely dedicated to her care and well-being, and that means that we have to present a *united* front. Intimacy between us will go a long way to helping us achieve that, I am certain. Now, go and have your bath and I will see you in the morning.'

It was only as he shut the door behind him, wincing in frustration at the desire that still held him in its taunting grip, that Nikolai recalled what Ellie had said to him at one of their earlier recent meetings. *'I was hurt and traumatised from the accident and for the first time in my life I let my father take charge and look after me.'* For a girl who had been raised the way she had— shunted from children's home to foster-home and back again—her father finally waking up to his responsibility and taking care of her when she had been hurt definitely struck a reluctantly sympathetic chord within Nikolai.

Arina could have suffered a similar fate if he had not been around to take her in when his brother had to all intents and purposes abandoned her after her mother's death. Nikolai knew Sasha had been traumatised by what had happened to Jackie, but why could he not have pulled himself together sufficiently to see that his daughter needed him? The thought that Arina could have suffered like Ellie must have suffered was like a knife score across his heart.

Returning to his room in a contemplative mood, he recalled how Ellie had flinched when Arina had asked if she had ever had shiny red shoes when she was small. The question must have speared deep into the heart of the child inside her who had been so cruelly and thoughtlessly abandoned by the very person who was supposed to love and protect her. But, no matter how much Nikolai might sympathetically regret Ellie's difficult upbringing, it didn't help to tamp down the wave of desire that flooded him every time he thought about her being naked under that thin little robe she'd been wearing…

The next morning, Ellie overslept. She didn't mean to, but as soon as her head had touched the pillow the night before, sheer emotional exhaustion had claimed her and she had yielded to it without so much as a whimper. *That almost never happened.*

Usually her mind was full of thoughts about her day—her clients' problems, and the kids at the shelter whose every day was a fight for survival and rarely anything anticipated with joy or pleasure—and Ellie would lie awake for at least an hour or two, sometimes even longer, mulling over them all, praying for ways in which she could do the most good and help them even more. To enjoy a deep, dreamless sleep was a gift she hadn't expected. And to anticipate a Sunday where she wouldn't have to work because she had moved house was another blessing.

Her thoughts turned to Arina and what the two of them could do that day. Maybe she could ask Miriam to make them up a picnic and they could spend the afternoon in Regents Park? It would be lovely to have some time to bond with the child on her own. The park was so close by, and they could walk there rather than get Nikolai's driver to transport them. The idea of a walk and a picnic galvanised Ellie into action.

Outside her window the day looked blustery and autumnal, and already the leaves on the giant oak were turning from a rich forest-green to a much lighter, burnished brown hue. Just perfect for the outing she had in mind! She dressed in jeans and a crisp white cotton shirt with a navy-blue sweater draped over her shoulders, and was almost at the door when her thoughts were suddenly ensnared by something else. Something she'd been trying so desperately hard not to dwell on. *Nikolai…*

As the tape of her memory anxiously played back what had happened between them last night, every muscle in her body locked almost excruciatingly tight. *'You will share my bed,'* he'd promised her and her mind and body had gone into meltdown at the mere idea. Frankly, it terrified Ellie that she was so acutely receptive to his touch. It seemed he only had to look at her a little longer than was necessary and she knew a frightening yearning for his hands to be on her body, her skin bare to his devastating attentions and her mouth plundered by his hot velvet kisses…

The needs he had accused her of having were obviously real—but apart from the fear in Ellie's mind that Nikolai would probably respect her even less, not more, if she easily succumbed to fulfilling them with him, there was something else that made her afraid to finally let down her guard. Something that filled her with the most tremendous anxiety and fear every time she thought about it…

She was *innocent…untouched…*had never experienced the ultimate intimacy with a man before…

CHAPTER NINE

In the spacious high-ceilinged kitchen, Arina and her father were already enjoying their breakfast at the scrubbed pine table when Ellie joined them. Miriam was busy arranging fresh toast in a silver rack, and as she brought it to the table she glanced up approvingly, her homely face wreathed in a smile. 'Good morning, Dr Lyons! Please sit down and I will get you your breakfast. Would you like a full English? Or perhaps you would prefer continental-style?'

It was hard to think about food when Ellie sensed Nikolai's arresting blue gaze immediately turn her way. He was dressed casually in jeans and a white T-shirt that stretched lovingly over smooth bronzed biceps that wouldn't put a trained athlete to shame, and the mouth-watering sight of so much blatant masculinity on show so early in the morning affected Ellie much more acutely than frankly was comfortable!

'Could I possibly just have some toast and marmalade and a cup of tea? I'm not really one for eating a lot in the morning. Thanks.'

'Good morning, Ellie,' Nikolai drawled. 'I trust you slept well?'

Ellie didn't think she'd imagined the slightly mocking overtone. 'I did, as a matter of fact...and you?'

'I am not generally a good sleeper, but as long as I have three or four hours I am fine.'

Three or four hours? And he could look as drop-dead gorgeous and vital as that? Ellie couldn't help but stare at him in awe.

'Sit down next to me, Ellie!' Arina patted the seat of the pine ladder-backed chair beside her, her pretty blue eyes shining with excitement and anticipation. 'Papa said we're going to the park today, and Miriam is going to make us a picnic!'

Great minds thinking alike, or some kind of weird telepathy? Ellie's stomach cartwheeled at the idea of Nikolai joining them on the trip she'd already been mentally planning as an opportunity for her to get to know her niece on her own. The fact was, like him or not, the man was just too distracting for words. How on earth was she supposed to be relaxed and at ease with him watching her every move and likely finding fault as well?

'Well... you'll never believe it, sweetheart, but I—' Just about to put her leather knapsack down on the floor beside her, Ellie heard the distinct sound of her mobile phone. The ringtone was Santana's 'Black Magic Woman,' and she sensed her cheeks flush hot pink as she caught Nikolai's eye and disconcertingly saw him smile. She bit her lip. 'I wouldn't normally answer it while we're eating but it might be work...do you mind?'

'Be my guest.'

Seeing immediately that it was Paul—the young colleague who helped run the shelter—Ellie felt her heart skip a beat.

'Hi. Did you forget today's my day off? Is anything the matter?'

'Sorry, Ellie, but I've got some bad news, I'm afraid.'

'Tell me!' Her stomach plummeting, Ellie tightly gripped the phone.

'Last night we were broken into. Nobody was hurt, thank God—most of the kids were all upstairs asleep when it happened. But the TV was stolen, along with most of the stuff that was any good in the kitchen—the toaster, the kettle and the microwave. They're all gone.'

'Oh, no!'

Furious and saddened at the same time—they'd only had a fundraiser very recently to replace all the items Paul had mentioned, because the previous ones had been so decrepit—Ellie assumed her usual 'take charge' mode. 'Did you ring the police?'

Nikolai glanced at her sharply.

'They've been here since the early hours, taking prints and so on. They are just about to leave.'

'Was there much mess?'

'Whoever it was trashed the place. It wasn't exactly Buckingham Palace before, but it's going to take a major miracle to make it anywhere near habitable again. They chucked a can of red paint up all the walls. Looks like a scene from a gangster movie!'

'Oh, Paul!'

'Don't upset yourself… We'll soon get it fixed up and shipshape again!'

The concern in Paul's kind voice almost undid her. The volunteers who worked alongside her were equally as committed to and caring of the inmates at the shelter as she was. This was a bitter blow for them too, and made a mockery of all their hard work.

Ellie rallied. 'Of course we will! Listen...I'm going to come in and take a look. Give me about an hour and I'll be with you. I'll have to get the tube. I'm not local any more.'

'Just get here when you can. I'll ring round a couple of the volunteers and get them to come in and help start cleaning up.'

'Thanks, Paul. See you.'

'Who is Paul?'

Ellie blinked at the distinct coolness in Nikolai's tone. 'He's a colleague of mine at the shelter.'

'The shelter?'

'It's a refuge we set up a few months ago for kids sleeping rough on the streets. Last night it got broken into and trashed. I'm sorry, but I'm going to have to go in for a little while and see for myself what's happened. Perhaps I can come and find you and Arina in the park afterwards? I'll ring you.'

'Is your commitment at the shelter not a voluntary one? How much time does it usually demand of you?'

Not having mentioned her work at the shelter to him personally, Ellie quickly realised that in spite of his question Nikolai must have found out about it when he had had her investigated. A wave of anger swept through her. *Was he going to tell her she had to end her association with the shelter*? Prepared to do battle on that score, Ellie felt her heart beat a little faster at what she judged to be disapproval in Nikolai's hard-jawed glance.

'I usually put in at least one or two hours each night after work,' she told him. 'Now that my situation has changed, I realise I may not be able to do that *every* night.'

'Is not enough of your time already given over to work, Ellie? You have a family to think of now, and that must take precedence!'

Glancing at Arina's bewildered little face, Ellie felt a huge stab of guilt shoot through her at the realisation that she *did* give an awful lot of her time to work—both paid *and* voluntary. Now that she was effectively going to become this child's mother she would have to cut back on certain commitments. It was only fair. Thinking of the planned picnic, and knowing only too well how acutely a child could feel disappointment if let down, she vowed to make it up to the little girl just as soon as she could.

Biting back a defensive retort to Nikolai, Ellie pushed her fingers through her thick blonde hair and sighed. 'The shelter helps a lot of young people who have nowhere else to go at night. It also helps keep them away from the thugs and the drug pushers that they often encounter during the day. I *will* cut back on my commitment there, but as for this morning—I'm sorry, but I'm just going to have to go over there and make an assessment of the damage. I'll try not to be too long, and I promise I'll come and join you both just as soon as I can.'

Saying nothing in reply, Nikolai got up and moved across the room towards the cream-coloured telephone on the wall, punching in a number. Whoever he was calling answered straight away. 'Ivan—' Ellie heard

him say, and then the rest of his speech was lost to her
as he continued the conversation in Russian. Replacing
the receiver, he glanced at the gold watch that glinted
on his tanned wrist before meeting her gaze again. 'I will
drive you myself to this shelter, and Ivan will accompany us.'

Shocked to her boots, Ellie stared. 'You don't have
to do that! I can easily get the tube.'

'I do not think you realise the position you are now
in. You are soon to become my wife! Not only does that
give you the right to expect my help when you need it,
but it also means that you do not take unnecessary risks
and possibly jeopardise yourself or this family in any
way! Ivan will be here in no time at all, and then we will
go. Miriam? The little one will have to stay with you
until our return. I will ring you to let you know when
we are on our way back.'

'Yes, Mr Golitsyn.'

'Arina?'

'Yes, Papa?'

'Stay with Miriam and help her make the picnic.
Ellie and I will not be away for very long, and then we
will all go to the park just as we planned my angel.'

'Yes, Papa.'

Not taking Ellie's advice to park the car a couple of
streets away, in case it was vulnerable outside the shelter, Nikolai grimly pulled in across the road from the
dilapidated building that was their destination. The expression in his eyes was steely as his gaze swept round
the litter-strewn pavements and the nearby houses with
their worn and neglected appearance.

His heart raced a little at the idea that Ellie should willingly expose herself to the volatile atmosphere of working in such a place. But inside him too was a reluctant admiration that she would make such a choice. It seemed to mock the fixed opinions he'd formed about her that he had convinced himself were right.

A small knot of disgruntled looking teenagers puffing away at rolled-up cigarettes—some with beer cans in their hands, and looking as if it had been months since they had had the use of soap and clean water—gathered round the shelter's entrance. A couple of them nodded their heads towards Ellie as she approached, Nikolai and Ivan close on her heels.

'Hear what happened, miss?' asked one of them—a thin youth with flattened brown hair and bloodshot eyes, his gaze warily straying behind her to the two men.

'That's why I'm here, Josh. Do you know anything about who could have done this?'

'No idea. Could've been anyone! Made a right bloody mess, though, whoever it was!' Visibly straightening his thin shoulders, Josh suddenly glared at Nikolai and his black-suited bodyguard. 'Who d'you think you are?' he mocked, clearly aiming for some kind of admiring recognition from his peers 'MI5? FBI?'

In the most seriously intimidating voice he could muster, Nikolai threw him an icy look. 'No. KGB,' he replied, and then, turning towards Ivan, said a few words in Russian.

The shock on the boy's face would have been quite comical if Nikolai hadn't been so impatient for Ellie to assess the damage inside and return home with him

again. The boy swore, and a second later moved aside
to let them all pass.

'You shouldn't have scared him like that!' Ellie ad-
monished Nikolai, but there was the smallest, disconcerting glimpse of humour at the corners of her mouth.
'Besides, weren't the KGB disbanded?'

Nikolai shrugged. 'He deserved it.'

As soon as they entered what seemed to be the
main living area, at the end of a scruffy hallway, they
saw that it did indeed resemble the film set of a
bloody gangster movie. The vivid red paint that
covered the walls was a shocking assault on the
senses, and glancing round at the smashed up furniture and crude messages on the patches of wall that
weren't submerged in scarlet Nikolai sensed a wave
of burning fury engulf him. This was no fit place for
Ellie to be! He wanted to take her by the shoulders
and march her out of there as swiftly as her shapely
legs would carry her!

But, seeing the desolation and sadness in her beautiful green eyes as she surveyed the stark evidence of
the break-in, he suddenly felt as protective of her as the
precious child he had adopted as his daughter. The
feeling genuinely took him aback...

'Oh, God!' She rubbed her hand over her cheek,
moving her head from side to side in anguish. 'Where
do we start to put this right?'

'Ellie... Hi...'

A young man with tousled fair hair, dressed in worn
denims and a black T-shirt, joined them. He barely
spared the two men with Ellie a glance before putting

his arm around her shoulders. Nikolai was instantly gripped by anger of a different kind.

'This is even worse than I imagined it would be, Paul!'

'I wanted to try and spare you too many details.'

'What did the police say?'

As though suddenly aware that Nikolai's intimidating gaze was taking unflattering measure of her young colleague, Ellie stepped slightly away from him and the man's arm dropped—reluctantly, it seemed to Nikolai—to his side.

'What could they say? You know how regularly this kind of thing happens round here! Just that they'll make the usual enquiries and get back to us when they have anything. In the meantime, I don't know how anyone can stay here with the place in this condition.'

'You're right. But where will they go?'

'On the streets…where they usually go. They'll manage. Give us a week or two and we might be able to get the place reasonably habitable again. But as for replacing the items that were nicked—I don't know how we're going to get those. By the way…who are your friends?'

'Oh… This is Nikolai and—'

'I am Ellie's fiancé.' Thinking he might as well put the man straight as soon as possible as to his relationship with Ellie, Nikolai moved protectively to her side.

'Fiancé?' Paul looked dumbfounded. 'You never said you were engaged!'

'It happened rather suddenly.' Giving him a weak smile, Ellie turned her gaze imploringly to Nikolai, as if to say *please don't say anything more*!

Did she have feelings for this man? he wondered jealously. Could his investigators have been wrong about her not having anyone she was interested in?

'What are these items that need replacing?' Forcing himself to change the subject, he immediately assumed authority.

'Most of our kitchen equipment and…' Ellie shrugged forlornly and Nikolai got the distinct impression that she was close to tears. 'What you see broken here. Most of the stuff was second-hand, but still… Anyway, I can replace most of the kitchen stuff. I can bring them from my flat, seeing as I'm not living there now.'

'You don't have to do that, Ellie.' Sounding irked, Paul narrowed his gaze almost accusingly as he surveyed the Russian. 'She's always giving us her own stuff or ploughing her own money into the shelter. It's not right!'

'Indeed, she should not have to do that,' Nikolai agreed, the faintest grim smile at the edges of his mouth. 'If you would make me a list of everything that needs replacing, I will see to it that it is taken care of. I will also arrange for a complete clean-up to be done of the property. Excuse me.'

Turning away from them all, Nikolai reached for the mobile phone in his jeans pocket and made a call. When he'd finished, he turned back to find Ellie staring at him in wide-eyed surprise. Right then he could not tell if she was pleased by his gesture or merely suspicious of it. But he just wanted to get her out of these stark and grim surroundings and back to somewhere more conducive to putting a smile on her lovely face again. *And if anyone could make her smile it would be Arina*, he thought proudly…

'A crew will arrive in about half an hour's time. They will see to everything.'

Shaking his head almost in disbelief, Paul replaced his scowl with a reluctant smile. 'This is very good of you, Mr…er…?'

'Golitsyn.'

'Right.' Still perplexed, Paul glanced at Ellie. 'Congratulations, by the way.'

She frowned. 'For what?'

'On your engagement!'

'Oh.' Her arresting emerald gaze moved warily back to Nikolai. 'Thanks.'

'Now it's Papa's turn to try and catch you, Ellie!' Clapping her small hands together with glee, Arina was clearly enjoying the game of tag she'd been playing with Ellie and her father. Relieved to put the problems of the shelter behind her for a while, Ellie was too.

It was the perfect day for spending time in the park, just as she had concluded earlier. The sun was shining, but there was a welcome cooling breeze, and the majestic trees surrounding them still shimmered with their raiment of leaves. However, the mere idea of a supremely fit and athletic Nikolai chasing her with the sole aim of catching her induced a heat in Ellie that was nothing to do with the exertion of the game.

A disconcerting awareness of the man's more physical attributes had been building in her all morning, and when he had accompanied her to the shelter and insisted on replacing all the items that had been stolen or broken, as well as arranging for the place to be professionally cleaned up, Ellie had helplessly found her unsettling attraction for him growing. *Despite* her automatic suspicions of his motives.

'Run, Ellie—run!' shouted Arina from beneath the large oak tree they'd been picnicking under. 'Papa's started counting!'

'Coming—ready or not!' her father proclaimed, with a definite lascivious glint in his eye, and Ellie pounded across the grass for all she was worth, despite being slightly disadvantaged by her limp.

To her immense frustration, she didn't get very far before an electric stirring of the air made all the hairs at the back of her neck stand up, warning her that Nikolai was right behind her. Arms with all the strength of iron bars pinioned her to his strong hard body, and Ellie's breath left her lungs in a disconcerting whoosh. Before she could get her bearings, Nikolai had pushed her to the ground. Just before she hit the earth he somehow arranged it so that he hit it first, and her fall was cushioned by his long, prone body.

Finding herself staring down into his teasing smiling face, into twinkling eyes as blue as the great dome that was the sky above them, Ellie was hardly aware that she breathed at all in those few electrifying seconds.

'Now I have you right where I want you, *laskovaya moya*!' he triumphantly declared—and kissed her.

As soon as Nikolai's lips touched hers, and his velvet tongue smoothly infiltrated Ellie's mouth, she melted and froze all at the same time. Suddenly he manoeuvred her body so that her denim-clad thighs were spread either side of his tight lean hips. Trying hard not to succumb to the prowess and danger of his slow, seductive kiss and failing dismally, Ellie became not only aware of the overwhelming effect he was having on her own aroused libido but also of how Nikolai's arrestingly fit body was so acutely responding to hers. His hardness pushed against her centre, and she gave a little yelp of shock mingled with a pleasure so fierce that her womb contracted and her nipples stung as though bitten.

Reluctantly, she stopped Nikolai kissing her. It seemed that the taste of him had not just infiltrated Ellie's mouth but the rest of her senses too, and she felt drugged, dizzy with a sensuality she hardly remembered was possible.

'Arina will see!' Ellie stared back at Nikolai in genuine alarm. If she had ever forgotten what his touch could do to her she had just been well and truly reminded and had good cause to be apprehensive of a repetition. Seducing her would be so easy for him she told herself. After all, it was a normal and even necessary function for a vital and healthy male specimen like him. But for Ellie it would be much, much more complicated…

'We are not doing anything to be ashamed of!' Easing himself up into a sitting position as she rolled away from him, Nikolai considered her with mocking amusement as he brushed some loose blades of grass from his jeans. 'I want her to see that we like each other and to feel secure in the fact.'

'*Like* each other? When did you decide that?'

'Would you prefer that I hated you?'

'Why change the habit of a lifetime?'

'I do not hate you, Ellie. What you did was unforgivable but I have since been reminded that you *do* have some admirable qualities... And I would be a liar if I said I was not attracted to you.'

'By "attracted" you mean you want to have sex with me?'

His shoulders went rigid for a moment, and his sensual lips compressed a little, as though he was offended. 'A crude way of putting it, perhaps—but, yes...I will not deny it!'

'And will that be in return for doing what you did today at the shelter?'

Now Nikolai was even more offended. 'What I did was a spontaneous gesture, not something planned to extract sexual favours from my wife-to-be!'

'Why did you help me?'

'I—'

'Papa—you caught her!'

Out of breath from running, Arina suddenly appeared beside them, her plump cheeks pink from exertion, clearly delighted at seeing them sitting so close together on the grass.

'Yes, angel.' Her father laughed, that devastating twinkle in his eye again as he turned his gaze back to Ellie. 'Unfortunately poor Ellie did not run fast enough!'

CHAPTER TEN

ELLIE sat in frozen animation on the floor, the boxes of books she'd started to open surrounding her. A searing knife-like pain had just throbbed through her skull, and in the midst of her unpacking she'd stopped still, willing it not to repeat itself. Assuring herself it was probably just a stress headache after what had happened at the shelter, she felt her breath catch at the disturbing scene that was starting to unfold in her mind—like a scroll she was slowly rolling opened to read the writing right to the end...

It was a repeat of the disturbing dream she had had about Sasha. But this time it went beyond the point where he was begging her to drive him to his friend's. His dark handsome face was contorted with frustration and irritation, and the baby was crying in his arms. He swore savagely beneath his breath, and then, realising he wasn't helping his case, regrouped himself and flashed Ellie one of his most disarming boyish smiles.

'What if I promise you that after this...after you drive me to my friend's...it will be the last time, the very *last* time, I ever take anything—drink or drugs—

and I ask Nikolai to get me some help? What if I do that, Ellie? It's what you've always begged me to do, isn't it? Give me this one last chance and I'll show you that I *can* get clean. Please, Ellie! Don't condemn me when I'm ill! Addiction is an illness, you must know that! My friend's place is only about a mile away. I want to see him because he's let me down, Ellie. He sold me some bad gear and I've got to speak to him!'

'Maybe you need to go to the hospital rather than your friend's, Sasha? What have you taken? What did he give you?' Alarmed, Ellie honestly feared for him if she left him to his own devices. He had a disturbingly frantic look in his eyes and clearly wasn't capable of making rational decisions right now. *If only he would ask Nikolai for help then everything could change*, Ellie thought fervently. Given time, he might even come round to seeing how precious and important his baby girl was, and at last forge a real loving bond with her just as Jackie would have longed for him to do.

Arina's cries turned to a snuffly whimper and Ellie longed to hold the child and comfort her.

'I don't need the hospital! I just need to see my friend and sort things out!' Sasha slurred, his balance wavering a little as he held the baby.

Ellie stared at him in horror. 'Give me Arina, Sasha… Let me take her and then we can get in the car and go. I promise I'll drive you, but let me take the baby first!'

'I am sorry, Ellie… But I need you to do this for me, and the baby is my insurance! Here are the car keys.' Sasha dragged them out of his jeans pocket and pressed them into Ellie's hand. 'Let's go.'

He marched towards Nikolai's smart gold coloured Mercedes parked kerbside, and she realised that he had taken his brother's keys. She had no choice but to hurry after him. Arina was her first and most urgent concern. She had to get her away from Sasha soon, before the worst happened and he dropped her!

The quiet street seemed to be free of passersby that afternoon, but even if she stopped someone for help there was no telling what Sasha might do in his current state of mind. *He was right*. He *was* ill. She didn't think she had ever seen him quite this bad before. So, with the car keys he had shoved into her trembling hand enclosed in her palm, Ellie climbed into the driver's seat, her gaze nervously on the wriggling baby in his arms, sick to her stomach at the volatile and potentially dangerous situation she found herself in.

'If I'm going to drive anywhere you need to put Arina in her baby seat. We can't travel with her on your lap. It's too dangerous. You absolutely *have* to do this!' she said firmly.

'Don't fret,' Sasha said impatiently. 'I'll put her in the car seat—don't worry. But then we've got to go.'

Swallowing hard, Ellie felt her hands clammy with fear as Sasha fumbled to get the baby in her car seat, then returned to the passenger seat and told Ellie to start driving.

'Have you strapped her in properly?' she demanded, twisting round to see for herself.

'Yes, yes!' Sasha replied. 'Now let's go!'

The scene started to fade, and—still kneeling on the carpet in her bedroom—Ellie pressed her palms to the sides of her face and briefly shut her eyes tight. She breathed out heavily. This time she knew what had just been revealed to her was no dream. It was pure shocking memory, and it had left her reeling, occurring out of the blue like that.

Knowing for certain that she had not willingly got into the car with Sasha that day, had only done so because he'd been high and she'd feared he might do himself or the baby harm if she didn't—Ellie felt immense relief roll through her. But how she would relate this unpalatable record of events to the man she had now agreed to marry she had no idea.

There was no doubt in her mind that Nikolai had loved his brother, despite all his faults—that was surely why he sought to avenge his death by blackmailing her, she realised. But the truth would surely test that love, and possibly make Nikolai feel more strongly than ever that he had somehow failed Sasha. Knowing the level of responsibility for his brother that he had always taken upon his shoulders, Ellie didn't doubt that. But being able to reveal the truth to him at last might not exactly endear Ellie to him either—for all that she'd longed for her memory to return.

From inside her bag, which lay on the bed, her mobile phone rang. Still in a bit of a daze, she jumped up to answer it. Having not rung her father yet, to tell him about the situation with Nikolai and that she had moved back into his house, Ellie thought for a worried moment that it might be him. But the caller was Paul from the shelter.

'Ellie? Just wanted to let you know that the cleaning crew your fiancé arranged turned up and did the most amazing job on the place you've ever seen! It looks even better than before. I know that's not saying much, but everyone here is over the moon! Say thanks from us all, will you?'

Dropping down onto the edge of the bed, Ellie clutched the phone to her ear with relief. Now at least the kids who'd been staying there would not have to sleep on the streets tonight. Nikolai had indeed done a wonderful thing.

She frowned at the wave of longing that suddenly swept through her at the thought of him, and her cheeks burned as she remembered that disturbing game of catch in the park, when he had caught her and kissed her…

'Of course I will,' she told Paul. 'I'm just so pleased the place is habitable again! It means we can think about our plans for improvement—as we'd hoped we could before this happened.'

'It's just a thought…but I wondered if you fancied meeting me for a quick drink? I'm in Leicester Square with a couple of friends of mine, and thought you might like the opportunity to celebrate everything turning out so well?'

Grateful for a chance to distract herself from thoughts of Nikolai, and the disturbing revelations about Sasha her returning memory had revealed, Ellie didn't hesitate to accept Paul's invitation. 'Sounds good. Give me about an hour and I'll join you. Where will you be?'

In the kitchen, having cleaned up after dinner, Miriam was having a final tidy round before she retired to her own rooms for the night.

'Miriam? Do you know where Mr Golitsyn is?' Ellie

asked, her heart thudding at the very real chance Nikolai might suddenly appear from wherever he'd gone after putting Arina to bed and take her by surprise. She had kissed the little girl goodnight earlier, after he had suggested Ellie might like to finish her unpacking.

'He has gone into his study to do some work, Dr Lyons…I mean Ellie.' The older woman smilingly grimaced, remembering that Ellie had told her to use her first name. 'He asked me to tell you that he would be busy for a couple of hours and to help yourself to anything you need in the meantime.'

Breathing a soft sigh of relief, Ellie released the blonde curl she had been absently twirling round her finger and did up the buttons on the three quarter-length jacket she wore over her jeans. 'Well, I've just had a phone call from a friend of mine, inviting me for a drink. If Nikolai wants to know where I've gone, would you tell him? I'd rather not disturb him if he's working.'

'Of course! I hope you have a nice evening.'

'Thanks very much… Goodnight, Miriam.'

'Good night, Ellie.'

It was useless trying to work when his concentration was shot to pieces! Why was he even bothering to attempt to read his letters when his secretary could look them over for him in the morning at his office?

Throwing down his fountain pen on the desk, Nikolai rose to his feet and circled his shoulders forwards and then backwards, moving his head from side to side to try and erase some of the strain in his ridiculously tense muscles. All his thoughts had been preoccupied with

Ellie…that was why he could not work. Deliberately removing himself from her company shortly after dinner, to read a bedtime story to Arina, he had told himself that some time spent without her lovely face and sultry perfume distracting him was just what he needed to help straighten out his mind about her.

Seeing the shelter today, and learning that it was Ellie who had set it up in the first place, had made Nikolai seriously reflect on why a girl he had accused of stealing a valuable necklace and aiming to run off with his charming but reckless brother would spend her time helping disadvantaged teenagers sleeping rough on the streets. It did not make sense. If she was only interested in acquiring money and living a more wealthy existence herself. The two behaviours just did not tally.

Doubt started to creep into his mind about Sasha's behaviour in the past. Had Nikolai overlooked too many of his less than charming character traits and perhaps extended him too much benefit of the doubt because he had felt so responsible for him and loved him? *With both their parents gone, what else could he have done*? Yet who knew what might have really occurred that fatal day of the accident? Thinking too about Ellie's obvious affection for Arina, Nikolai felt something deep down inside him telling him that what she had said was true…*She would never have knowingly or willingly put the child at risk*…Not even for Sasha, if she'd cared for him!

Shaking his head, he uttered her name out loud in sheer frustration. His body throbbed with the need to hold her, and that kiss they had shared earlier in the park had only poured petrol on the fire that already simmered hotly inside him. If he did not get her into his bed soon he might have to seriously consider ringing up one of his previous lovers after all! He knew that he wouldn't. Since seeing Ellie again it was impossible for him to even *think* of being intimate with someone else.

There was a knock at the door. Scraping his fingers through his hair, Nikolai found himself tensing even more at the idea it might be Ellie. When he saw his small rotund housekeeper in her wrap-around floral apron standing there instead, in the softly lamplit hall, disappointment crashed in on him like a wave.

'Yes, Miriam?'

'I have a message for you from Ellie, Mr Golitsyn.'

'Well?' he snapped impatiently. 'What is it?'

'She has gone out for a while with a friend. She did not want to disturb you. As I was just on my way up to bed, I thought I had better come and tell you.'

'Who is this friend? Did you see him or her?'

'No, Mr Golitsyn.'

'When did she leave?' Nikolai demanded, his mind and heart racing at the idea that Ellie might be running out on him and Arina again, and berating himself for starting to see the good in her instead of the bad.

'About half an hour ago, Mr Golitsyn.'

'And you are sure she did not mention who this friend was?'

'No. I am sorry.'

Wishing that Miriam had come and told him all this earlier, still Nikolai realised he could not blame his good-hearted housekeeper for Ellie going out. And in spite of the agreement they had made he could hardly keep her prisoner in what was now her home...*could he*? Yet the steel-like muscles in his stomach cramped painfully at the idea that she had gone out with some unknown male admirer.

'Go to bed, Miriam. I will wait up for Ellie. Sleep well.'

'Yes, Mr Golitsyn.' Unable to banish the concern that she had somehow done something wrong, the housekeeper sighed and lifted her shoulders in a resigned shrug.

'Did you have a nice evening?'

Rising from the armchair he had been sitting in whilst waiting for her return, Nikolai did not know how he managed to keep his tone so calm and civilised. It was after midnight, and he had endured wave upon wave of fear and doubt that Ellie had left him for good.

Perhaps she had concluded that it was worth the risk of her and her father going to prison after all to get away from Nikolai? Now, his worsening mood poised on a precarious knife-edge, he let his gaze flick in reluctant and helpless admiration over her appearance. With the lamp light from the hallway outside the sitting room wreathing her hair in a halo of gold, in contrast her pale skin appeared almost luminous—whilst her emerald eyes glinted like dark fire as they registered her surprise at seeing him.

'Nikolai! You didn't need to wait up for me. It's late, and I have the key you gave me to let myself in.'

'Where have you been?'

'Didn't Miriam tell you?' Ellie frowned, 'A friend of

mine rang and invited me out for a drink. I would have told you myself, but you were working and I didn't want to disturb you.'

'And this friend of yours...Was it male or female?'

'What?'

'You heard me perfectly well, I am sure.'

'I don't believe this! Are you going to cross-examine me every time I set foot outside the door? Maybe next time you'll make me take Ivan as well! Then you can spy on who I'm with and keep me prisoner all at the same time!'

His temper finally spilling over, Nikolai swore savagely beneath his breath, his hands clenched into fists of tension and fury down by his side. 'You go too far!'

'No!' She took several strides towards him and jabbed her finger in the air. 'It is *you* who go too far!'

Reacting instinctively, Nikolai caught her slender-boned wrist and gripped it tight.

She gasped. 'Let go of me!'

Seeing fear in her eyes, he stared at her in stark cold horror as he realised she thought he was going to strike her. Before he could let her go, her face crumpled, and she moved her hand across her eyes to hide her distress. Again, acting purely on instinct, adrenaline pumping through his veins like white water, Nikolai impelled Ellie urgently into his arms.

'I wasn't going to hurt you. I swear to you I would cut off my hand before I laid it on you in anger, *devochka moya!*' *My little girl...* It was the same endearment he used sometimes when speaking to Arina, and it had slipped out quite naturally.

Nikolai's hand was smoothing over the silken fall of Ellie's alluring shampoo-scented hair—faint notes of sandalwood and orange—and, unable to resist, he kissed the top of her head... Once, twice, three times. The contact only deepened his frustration and desire. It was nowhere near enough to satisfy the building need in him for complete fulfilment...not when his lips ached to kiss and taste and explore every exquisite inch of her and his body longed to be one with hers. If previously Nikolai had been angry, then what he was experiencing right now was light years away from that emotion and silently, devastatingly, it shook him to his very foundations.

Trembling, Ellie pressed herself closer into his chest with a sigh. 'One of my foster fathers hit me across the face once when he was angry...I've never forgotten it.'

'I am sorry that you experienced such brutality from a man who should have protected you...Let me assure you that I would never, *never* do such a thing to you!'

'I know...'

Softly pliant and warm, and no longer defensive, Ellie let her hands come to rest either side of Nikolai's hips. Even though her touch was feather-light, it burned through the tough material of his jeans. Volcanic heat pulsed through his bloodstream and made him hard. Cupping her face, he let his hungry gaze briefly scorch her before he lowered his mouth and claimed her softly opened rose-pink lips in a kiss that transported him far from this world... 'Come with me...' his voice beseeched her, when he could finally bear to tear his lips away from the sweet wild honey taste of hers. 'Come with me, and for a few hours we will shut out the world and think only of each other.'

CHAPTER ELEVEN

FINDING herself in a situation she had both feared and yet secretly longed for, Ellie let her nervous gaze move slowly round Nikolai's sumptuously designed bedroom, with its silk wallpaper and antique furniture. She heard the ominous click of the door shut behind her. Sensing his eyes burning into her back in the way that she'd often found him studying her—with the most disturbing and yet heart-stopping intensity—she felt her mouth go dry and a quiver of excitement ripple through her.

It was hard to take her own eyes off the stately and astonishing four-poster bed that loomed up in front of her. Complete with mirrors in the headboard, and enough brocade and silk cushions on top of the luxurious purple counterpane to please Cleopatra herself, surely it was a bed made for seduction? *What was she thinking of?*

Ellie grimaced at her own question. The problem was that she *wasn't* thinking. Her brain was not the part of her anatomy she was engaging at all! All she knew was that this man made her feel something deep and powerful…something she hardly *dared* to feel… And she wanted—no, *needed* to sample more of that spell-binding sensation. It might not make any sense to an outsider, given their past traumatic history together, and yet there it was.

All through the evening spent with Paul and his two cheerful companions she had hardly been able to think about anything but Nikolai, immersed in his work again. Didn't he ever long to make a real connection with someone? she'd thought, almost desperately. With Arina and work his two main priorities, had he relegated any hopes he might have had for a deeper relationship with a woman to a completely lost cause? After all, he had strongly asserted that he was only interested in a marriage of convenience now, after his first marriage had failed so miserably.

All evening the strongest impulse to return to the house and be with him had been building inside Ellie. Despite his anger towards her over the past—despite all of that—she knew something inside him was trying to reach out to her, and from the moment she had seen him again, she had been slowly and inevitably moving towards that call.

She turned round to face him. 'This is a lovely room.'

Nikolai smiled at the comment. And this time the only danger reflected in that riveting gesture was the se-ductive promise that glinted in his eyes and lingered round the edges of his compelling mouth. 'Made all the lovelier by your presence, my angel.'

Struck dumb as he approached her, it seemed to Ellie that every inch of her skin was alive with the sensation of his touch—even though he hadn't physically made contact with her yet.

Also silent, Nikolai reached out for her, to slide his arm round her waist and lift her up high against his chest as easily as if her weight amounted to nothing. His glance boring into hers like simmering blue flame, he laid her down on the sumptuous bed, and with another enigmatic smile drew his hand lightly down the centre of her chest.

Ellie gasped as one by one he flicked open the three half-moon-shaped mother-of-pearl buttons on her blouse, discovering that she had a penchant for very feminine underwear. She saw the pleasure in his sexy blue eyes deepen as they skimmed the semi-sheer floral bra she was wearing, with its pink satin bow in the centre and prettily decorated straps.

Murmuring, 'Beautiful…' Nikolai reached behind Ellie's slim back and undid the fastening.

When his hands palmed her exposed breasts she bit her lip and briefly closed her eyes, hardly prepared for the storm of need that rippled hotly through her. When he pinched her aching, tingling nipples and sublime languorous heat invaded her—the aroused velvet tips surged hotly into his hands and made her gasp again.

Leaning back to shrug off his shirt, Nikolai smiled lazily. Getting the distinct message that he planned to take his time making love to her, and would relish every moment, Ellie sighed, surprisingly content and quite prepared to wait. After all, what did she have to complain about? Just the sight of him was a feast for the senses.

Bare-chested now, he was long bodied and lean-waisted, with heavenly broad shoulders that she longed to rest her head against. The sight of his golden-tanned torso, silky smooth and perfect, with its mouthwatering display of toned lean muscle and smattering of dark blond hair over flat male nipples, made another surge of heat flow into Ellie's already melting centre, and her thighs quivered to contain it.

'Now we have to get rid of some of these clothes, don't you think?' Smiling like the cat that got the cream, Nikolai peeled off his own jeans and then Ellie's.

While she still reeled with the new sense of urgency and demand in his touch, he covered her near naked body with his and kissed her. It was the most deeply erotic and exploratory kiss she had ever encountered. Her senses were already saturated with the clean, yet musky warm scent of the man as his hard body pressed her down into the bed—and the taste of him was like hot summer nights under the stars. Ellie could have wept with pleasure.

What Nikolai did not know was that no man had ever held her this intimately before—but very soon he would find out. A small stab of unease stole away her joy for the briefest moment, but then her lover moved his sensuous velvet mouth from hers onto her breasts, and she forgot everything but the sheer ecstasy that she was drowning in.

Her hands were moving over his body too, in an instinctive need to give him back some of the pleasure he was giving her. As her palms cupped the tight smooth buttocks beneath his black silk shorts, she felt them clench and his sex—already like steel against her belly—seemed to grow even harder. Emitting a sound that was very like a satisfied growl, he lifted his head, gave her a wicked smile, then kissed her passionately on the mouth, his tongue thrusting hotly inside her.

Disengaging himself only temporarily, Nikolai started to inch Ellie's delicate floral panties down over her hips and then with the minimum of fuss deftly removed his shorts. Kissing her again, as though he could scarcely bear being apart from her for even a second, he slid his hand down between their bodies over the soft tiny curls between her quivering thighs. While Ellie was absorbing this new, fiercely erotic delight he stroked his fingers across her hot moist centre. She sighed out her pleasure and shock on a husky breath.

The feelings that this most intimate of touches elicited were so intense that shuddering emotion brought tears to her eyes. It was frightening to sense all her defences being as expertly and vividly demolished as they were being now. Vulnerability was always scary, but she was so tired of being numb with grief and pain and regret. To feel *anything* was surely better than that?

Now Nikolai was murmuring to her in Russian, and it was the sexiest sound Ellie had ever heard, even though she didn't know what his words meant. Her hands moved tenderly over his short fair hair and round the rough coating of stubble that studded his hard jaw.

'What are you saying?' she asked softly, with a helpless catch in her voice as he inserted a finger deep inside her. Her muscles tightened in shock around him.

'I am saying,' he began, 'that you look and feel and taste like heaven to me, my bewitching, lovely Ellie... And that...' he spread her a little more with his fingers and she gasped '...I want to be inside you...right now.'

As he positioned himself at the apex of her thighs and started to slowly inch himself inside her Ellie knew great relief that Nikolai didn't just thrust into her without care, thinking only of his own urgent need for satisfaction. It made her heart swell with tenderness towards him even more. But she couldn't help but freeze for a moment as he started to fill and stretch her, and he glanced down at her with the faintest suggestion of a frown on his handsome face.

'I am not hurting you?' he asked with concern.

'No.' Her smile was quick to reassure him.

'Then it has been a long time, perhaps?' He frowned again.

Unable to bear the idea that he clearly thought she had shared her body with other men before him... namely his *brother*...Ellie reached out to touch his cheek. 'I'm fine, Nikolai...really. It's just that—'

'What?' Now his whole body stiffened, and he stopped moving inside her, the honed muscles in his biceps taut as iron as he held himself above her.

'I've never been with a man like this before,' she breathed, anxiety making her bite her lip.

'You have *never*? You are telling me you are innocent?'

'Yes.'

Would he stop making love to her now that he knew the truth? Perhaps even believe she was using her virginity as some kind of manipulative tool?

But Nikolai wasn't regarding her with disapproval at all. Instead there was the most beguiling smile hovering about his delectable lips.

'You are so beautiful,' he murmured, before claiming her mouth in another all-consuming and avid kiss.

Slowly he started to move inside her again, encouraging her to wrap her firm, shapely legs around that perfect lean waist of his, so that he could go deeper. Surprised, and secretly delighted at how her body responded so meltingly to his possession, realising that pain had hardly featured at all, Ellie finally allowed her tense body to relax. *It would be all right.* This was a totally natural and beautiful experience between a man and a woman. It was only her past anxieties around men in general that had made her resist sampling it before. *But then no man she had ever met apart from Nikolai had made her want to surrender her virginity before.*

Giving herself up to the sensations of joy and ecstasy that were building like a storm about to break inside her as Nikolai's thrusts became more rhythmic and urgent, it was Ellie who confidently and eagerly sought his mouth and claimed it. Soon after that her huskily voiced gasps littered the air as wild sensation dissolved into never-before-imagined bliss.

As she fought to gain purchase on the torrent of emotions that engulfed her, her lover held himself still above her, groaned out loud, then slowly lowered himself against Ellie's chest as she registered a sensation of scalding heat and dampness drench her insides. As he cupped her face, his blue eyes had never regarded her with such searing scrutiny before.

'Why did you wait so long to be with a man?' he asked.

'I've never met a man I wanted to be with like this before…that's why.' For Ellie there was no conflict involved whatsoever.

'Not even my brother?' Nikolai's gaze was fierce again, and she saw doubt and deep inner turmoil flit across the brilliant azure irises.

'I was never with Sasha in an intimate situation—and I was certainly never attracted to him either!'

'I have been tormented these past five years, thinking of you and him together in just such a situation as this!'

'But now you *know* that can't be true!' Ellie's chest was tight with fear that Nikolai would somehow not believe she'd been a virgin after all. She was also stunned to learn of his torment about her and his brother, and to hear such jealousy in his voice.

Sighing heavily, he moved his hands into her silken blonde hair. 'Yes… I know that you were innocent until you gave yourself to me just now. It is a gift no man should take for granted, *angel moy*, and it was wonderful! It makes me more certain than ever that it is right you should become my wife.'

Why? Because he wanted to possess her? *Own* her instead of *love* her? Her heart hurt at the very idea. Surrendering her innocence to Nikolai had been no small thing for Ellie. And now she had to face the most unexamined but possibly terrifying idea of all… She loved him—and on some deeply shocking level she knew that she *always* had.

'Why did you break up with your first wife?' she

asked, aware that she was potentially ruining something precious by stirring up the past again.

But she wanted to know about Nikolai and Veronika—the woman who had seemed to have made him so cynical and hard about marrying for love again.

Rolling away from her to lie on his back, Nikolai stared up at the ceiling. Feeling chilled without the warmth of his heavenly body, Ellie pulled an edge of the silk counterpane across her breasts.

'She was unfaithful to me...maybe more than once. I was away working a lot of the time, and she did not always want to come with me. You must have been aware when you came to live here after your sister died that my marriage was a sham. It had been over for a long time, really. When I look back now, I wonder how I could ever have chosen such a woman to be my wife! Apart from our Russian heritage we never did have very much in common. But I was young when I met her, and she acted like I hung the moon!' He lifted a shoulder. 'I suppose I fooled myself she was genuinely in love with me, and with all the responsibility of the family business thrust upon me I needed an ally. I was looking for a companion and friend as well as a lover Ellie...'

Turning his head, Nikolai studied her closely. Ellie wanted to say to him *You're so far away, lying over there... come back to me...* But because she had no certainty of anything right then as far as their relationship was concerned she held back the words.

'I'm sorry for the pain she must have put you through,' she said softly instead, genuinely meaning it.

His eyes widened. 'You never cease to astonish me—do you know that? You always seem to be thinking about somebody else's suffering and not your own! Why is that?'

'I don't particularly want to dwell on my own pain. I've sought to come to terms with it as best as I can, but I decided long ago that the past wasn't a good place to live and it was better to concentrate on trying to build a healthier future instead.'

'I feared that you would die when you were in the hospital.'

As he leaned up on an elbow, Nikolai's glance was grave and concerned. Her heart turning over in surprise and sorrow, Ellie sat up too. 'No!' she exclaimed. 'I was hurt badly, yes... But I knew I would recover. I'm a survivor, Nikolai. I *do* know that about myself.'

As soon as the words were out of her mouth she flinched—because Sasha had *not* survived. *Would Nikolai resent her for that for ever?* How would they make this planned marriage between them work if he could never let go of blaming her?

Thinking about the memory that had partially come back—no doubt stimulated by her return to this house—Ellie felt her stomach knot painfully at the idea of telling him just *why* she had been in the car with Sasha that day. *He'd loved his brother so much, and he'd already suffered such great torment and grief over his death.* Even if it meant exonerating herself at last, she was still torn about telling Nikolai what she now knew to be the truth about the events of that day.

'I saw you limping the other day, when I picked you

up from the studios,' he remarked thoughtfully. 'Did the surgery leave any scars?'

Tucking some hair behind her ear, feeling suddenly shy, Ellie held the edge of the sheet over her breasts as though it were a life-raft. 'It did...but they're actually not too bad.' Smiling, she moved some of the fabric away from her legs to reveal the two long scars that were about half an inch in width, running up the front of each bare, shapely thigh.

There was also one at the side of the ankle she had broken too. That was the cause of her limp. The surgeon concerned had done a fantastically neat job of sewing her up again after the operation, and Ellie had never wasted time fretting over the appearance of her scars. That had partly been because up until now—until she'd known for certain she had not voluntarily got into the car with Sasha and taken Arina with her—she had been racked with such terrible guilt and thought she'd deserved them.

Now Nikolai was touching each pale pink slightly raised blemish in turn, gently stroking his fingers across the tight repaired skin, his fascinating cheekbones appearing even more hollow and defined as his gaze became almost hypnotised by what he was viewing.

'Now it is my turn to tell you that I am sorry you endured so much pain...I truly regret that. But the truth is, Ellie, there is nothing that could spoil such incandescent beauty as yours...nothing!'

The hands that were touching her were suddenly coaxing her trembling thighs apart, running up the insides of them with renewed mesmerising purpose.

Shivering, Ellie barely had time to register her surprise when Nikolai ripped away the silk that she was modestly covering her nakedness with and covered her trembling form with his body instead.

'Now that I have you right where I want you I find that I cannot get enough of you! Something that I secretly always knew would be the case!'

And his velvet tongue slid in between the moist seams of Ellie's quivering mouth and made her forget both the past *and* the future, to concentrate vividly and unequivocally on the present…

The hands that covered the soft leather of the steering wheel were damp and slightly shaking. All through the nightmare car journey through London's busy traffic Ellie drew on every resource she had—mental, physical and emotional—to get her through the dreadful ordeal. Once they reached Sasha's friend's house she told herself that she would seize the chance…*any* chance…to get Arina safely away and back home to Nikolai—to the man she knew loved her more than he loved his own life.

But the alcohol and drugs he had taken were seriously messing with Sasha's head, and all through the drive he had been alternately muttering and then falling into a trance. Ellie seriously feared for him if she left him with this so-called friend, but she would cross that bridge when she came to it. Right now, for Arina's sake if no-one else's, she simply *had* to focus all her concentration on the road ahead.

She was momentarily and shockingly distracted when Sasha suddenly grabbed the wheel, babbling something about someone trying to get him, and shouting in terror. Frantically trying to get back control of the careening vehicle, Ellie inadvertently veered to the right of the queue of traffic in front of her. Before she could straighten the wheel she had to deliberately yank it even further right as an oncoming Land-Rover headed straight for them. Suddenly they were motoring towards a nearby lamppost instead.

From that moment on, time had taken on a sloweddown almost dream-like quality…and Ellie had watched events unfold as though she was an observer looking down on the scene instead of being part of it herself. The last thing she remembered was Sasha yelling and Arina crying, and then…and then *nothing*.

Merciful blackness had descended like a stormy raincloud blocking out the sun, and the next thing she recalled was waking up in hospital with the too-harsh lighting on the ceiling almost blinding her with its vulgar and painful intrusion…

'Sasha!' she cried out loud—a final picture flashing through her mind of his head slumped forward onto the dashboard covered in blood.

With her heart beating as if it would beat right out of her chest, Ellie opened her eyes to discover she had been dreaming, and was still in the opulent bed she had been sharing with Nikolai for most of the night.

But it was not just a distressing dream, she realised… It was the full and complete return of her memory of what had happened that day—and why the accident had occurred.

Pressing her hands either side of her head, Ellie

couldn't help murmuring beneath her breath… 'Dear God!' Now a little more conscious, she glanced round. Disturbingly, there was no sign of her attentive and ardent lover. All that remained of his presence was the sexy aroma of the aftershave that he wore and—as she discovered, touching the sheet—the warm imprint where his body had so recently been…

CHAPTER TWELVE

SHE HAD been calling out for Sasha again. Finding himself disturbed beyond belief as he had watched Ellie tossing her head from side to side and whimpering like a child in a way that rent his heart in two, Nikolai had finally got out of bed, pulled on his discarded jeans and silently left the room.

She had sworn to him that there had been nothing intimate between her and his brother, but even having found to his shocked surprise that she was indeed innocent, still Nikolai found himself wondering if she had secretly nurtured feelings for him. Why else would she dream about him so often? he asked himself. *And why else would she have willingly got into the car with him that day and taken Arina with her?*

Gripped by frustration at having no answers to any of these questions, and feeling an increasing sense of despondency that he never would, Nikolai made his way to the drawing room. He went to the drinks cabinet and poured out a generous measure of cognac. Tipping it down his throat in one hit, he grimaced at the burn that seared his stomach, but welcomed the temporary relief of pain it brought with it. It seemed he was destined to fall for women who found it impossible to love him just for himself and not feel they yearned to be with somebody else.

Shocked by the thought, and disparaging of the uncharacteristic wave of self-pity that washed over him, Nikolai moved barefooted across the elegant moonlit room and placed his empty glass on the white marble sill of the mantelpiece. Ellie's evocative scent still clung to him, and the realisation made him grow hot all over and instantly hard. She had been the most responsive and exciting lover, and Nikolai had revelled in teaching her the many ways of loving... What he had told her was true. He *had* always known that when he eventually made love to her it would never be enough. He had known it very soon after she had come to the house to be Arina's nanny, he remembered. There'd been something about her smile and her innocence that had bewitched him from the start. So much so that he had found himself seeking out her company whenever he was home, finding excuse after excuse to be in the same room as her and Arina, and fantasising about them becoming a 'real' family. *It had been his secret wish, and he had revealed it to nobody.*

Not until that evening in his office, when Ellie had brought him tea and somehow they had found themselves in each other's arms—not until then had he believed he might be able to turn his secret wish into a reality. But the next day all his hopes had been devastatingly smashed by the car crash that had stolen his brother's life, endangered his baby daughter and not only wounded Ellie but revealed her—so he had believed at the time—to be a liar and a thief.

Now, remembering his visit to the shelter for street kids she had set up, and witnessing the level of devotion she had to both the people who used it as well as the volunteers who worked there, he could not see how she could possibly be *either* of the uncomplimentary things he had accused her of being... Yet how could he trust her unless he knew for sure? He had been betrayed by a woman before, and it had left him feeling both bitter and wary of entering into another similar relationship. More to the point...could he trust revealing his heart to Ellie if she really had loved Sasha and preferred him to Nikolai?

'I've been looking for you.'

Caught up in his thoughts, Nikolai had not registered the soft creak of the door opening. Now he saw Ellie, barefoot and robed in that thin pink wrap he had seen her in before, regarding him with an expression on her lovely face that seemed uncertain and maybe even a little shy...

'I could not sleep,' he said gruffly, spearing his hand through his hair.

'Did I disturb you?' Closing the door behind her, Ellie hugged her arms over her chest and slowly walked towards him.

Outside, a full moon was shining. There was no need for lamplight or other light of any kind with the brightness it bestowed on the room. With her long blonde hair curling over her shoulders, her radiant skin and soft green eyes, she resembled a vision of loveliness and purity that took Nikolai's breath away.

'Yes, you disturbed me.' He smiled ruefully. 'But then you always do.'

'That's not what I meant.' Was that a blush he glimpsed seeping into her pretty cheeks? 'I was talking in my sleep...I might even have cried out,' she continued, looking torn.

Slowly Nikolai inclined his head. 'You called out for Sasha,' he told her, his heartbeat suddenly picking up to an uncomfortable speed.

'Most of my memory has come back.'

'*What*?'

'It must have been returning to this house that prompted it... I've been having dreams about what happened that day. Not just dreams, sudden memory recall too. I was going to tell you...'

'What do you remember?' The question had almost got lodged in Nikolai's throat he was so tense about the answer.

'What I'm about to tell you...you might not want to hear.'

Rubbing the flat of his hand across his bare ribcage, Nikolai sighed. 'What you consider I may or may not want to hear should not prevent you from telling me the truth, Ellie. Just come right out and say it.'

She stared at him for some time before uttering a word...as if she was considering how best to reveal what had to be said. When she finally started speaking there was a new look in her eyes, he noticed. A look that seemed more determined and resolved.

'You remember that Sasha had been drinking that day, before you left to go to your office?'

He moved his head in a brief nod.

'Well…what you may not have known was that he was high on drugs too. He had been taking them for some time…maybe at first to help him get over Jackie…who knows? Anyway, he begged me not to tell you about it. That afternoon, after you'd gone, he was agitated about getting to his friend's house—I think he was a dealer, Sasha said that he'd given him something bad…' Ellie flinched.

'He said he had to speak to him, and he pleaded with me to take him there. He said he would get a cab if I didn't, but I saw he was in no fit state to go anywhere alone, and I was worried that someone might find out who he was—that he was related to *you*, Nikolai—and the press would be on you like a ton of bricks! He was holding Arina and she was crying. He told me that she was his "insurance" to make sure I drove him where he wanted. He was really off balance, and I feared he might drop her. I had no choice but to agree to drive him. I made sure Arina was strapped into the car seat and we left. All the way Sasha was muttering, sounding more and more distressed. I realised then that I couldn't leave him alone with this supposed friend of his, and that I would have to do something—get help in some way. But I had to concentrate on driving safely—particularly because Arina was with us.' She bit her lip and glanced momentarily down at the floor. 'I think he might have been having hallucinations of some kind.'

Nikolai's stomach sickeningly turned over. 'What happened then?'

Ellie's hand touched her throat, and she seemed to

turn even paler in the moonlight streaming in through the opened window. 'All of a sudden he cried out and grabbed the wheel. He was muttering something about someone trying to get him. The car was swerving badly all over the road. I tried to get back control but he wouldn't let go of the wheel. All of a sudden I saw that a large four-by-four was heading towards us. With all my strength I managed to yank the wheel to the right, but that left us heading towards a lamppost by the side of the kerb. I don't remember much else after that, except waking up in hospital.'

Biting back the strong curse that hovered on his lips, Nikolai sucked in a breath and held it for a couple of seconds before audibly releasing it. *How blind could one man be*? he thought, anguished. Why had he not seen that Sasha was more addicted than he'd realised? And not just to alcohol but to drugs too?

Ellie was regarding him with an anguished look in her eyes. 'I'm sorry, Nikolai… Sorry that you had to find out such a shocking thing only now.'

For a long while Nikolai said nothing. Somehow words seemed woefully inadequate to begin to describe what he was feeling. He had received the most appalling shock—but part of him was already blaming himself for not seeing the truth long before. Had his sense of responsibility and his love for his brother prevented him from acknowledging that he might be numbing his pain with something other than drink? Why hadn't he moved heaven and earth to get him the help that he needed? Instead Nikolai had sought refuge from his own pain in work and in taking care of Arina, and in the meantime Sasha's addiction had got out of control and become potentially dangerous. In not seeing what was going on Nikolai had endangered both his daughter *and* Ellie. The shame and regret that pulsed through him in that instant knew no bounds.

'Nikolai, are you all right?' Stepping closer to him, Ellie reached for his hand. He could see by her expression that its icy temperature shocked her. He smiled grimly. 'Right now? No… I fear it may take quite some time before I am all right again after what I have just heard.'

'I've told you the truth. I swear it!'

'Do not distress yourself, my beautiful Ellie. You can rest assured that I believe everything you have said. It has come as a great shock, yes… But what has shocked me more is that I *knew* my brother was a potential danger to himself and those around him when he drank and lost control, and I did not persuade him hard enough to get some help. If I had known he was hooked on drugs too then I would have tried even harder! I took Arina under my wing because I loved her, but I did not protect *you* as I should have done, Ellie. I cannot begin to tell you how much I regret that.'

'You loved him,' she said softly, her emerald eyes shining as she glanced up at him. 'And you acted out of the best of intentions.'

Reaching out, Nikolai tipped up her chin. 'Is there no end to your capacity to forgive?' he asked huskily.

'Most people are only doing the best that they know how to do,' she answered. 'Blaming and holding grudges only brings more pain. Why are you smiling?'

'I am smiling, Ellie, because I am in awe of your

virtue, and I find myself wondering how a mere mortal man can ever deserve or live up to such a woman as you?'

'I'm no saint! I have plenty of flaws and faults, just like anyone else!' She frowned. 'There is something else I wanted to say.'

'Go on.'

'I don't know how that necklace got into the car, but I absolutely *know* that I did not steal it, Nikolai—and neither was my father involved in any way!'

Lifting a shoulder, he dropped his hand to his side. 'I believe you. It is clear as day to me that Sasha must have taken it—*and* all those other things that went missing from time to time. A drug habit is expensive…no matter how much money you have! Our argument was mainly over money, and he knew that I kept the necklace in my room. He must have taken it before he came downstairs to find you and demand that you take him to see this friend of his.' Moving away from Ellie, Nikolai released a resigned and weary sigh. 'You are absolved of all blame in everything I have ever accused you of. As of this moment you are free to leave, whenever you desire.'

'Leave?' Ellie echoed in shock, her beautiful eyes wide.

'Yes.' Nikolai held her gaze for a long and anguished moment. 'And you will of course be compensated for all the distress I have unwittingly caused you…*substantially*. I will not prevent you from seeing Arina whenever you want. Now I think we should both go back to our respective beds and get some sleep. We can talk about this again in the morning, if there is time before you leave to go to work. Good night, Ellie.'

Unable to look at her for a second longer without acting on his overwhelming desire to sweep her up into his arms and carry her straight back to his own bed, Nikolai walked to the door with a heavy tread and went out, leaving her standing there…

'Ellie, I did a beautiful picture of you and I made you into a princess!'

'Did you, darling? Let me see!'

Sipping the fragrant Italian coffee Miriam had kindly given her when she'd arrived in the kitchen earlier, Ellie felt her heart leap with pleasure at the sight of the little girl dressed in her green and grey school uniform. Having tried to prepare herself for Nikolai walking through the door at any moment, anticipating his arrival with a mixture of longing and trepidation after their abrupt parting in the early hours, she bit back her disappointment when it was Elsa she discovered close on the child's heels instead.

The blonde au pair greeted her with a cheerful smile. 'Good morning!'

'Good morning. Now, Arina…you must come and sit on my lap and show me this wondrous picture you have done of me!' Giving the child's drawing her full attention once she had climbed up onto her lap at the breakfast table, Ellie felt a wave of overwhelming emotion grip her when she saw with what care and loving detail the portrait had been composed.

Ellie had been drawn wearing a long sparkling yellow dress, with her wrists adorned in bright jewelled bracelets. On her head resided a crown decorated at regular intervals with what she guessed were meant to be emeralds. Her hair was long and rippling—the same butter-yellow as her dress—whilst her lips were candy-pink and her eyes the most startlingly bright green Ellie had ever seen!

'Oh, sweetheart!' she exclaimed, giving the little body on her lap a warm, heartfelt hug, 'This is amazing! Nobody told me we had such an incredible artist in our midst!'

'I'm glad you like it, Ellie.' Jamming her thumb into her mouth in a sudden fit of shyness, Arina looked flushed with pride at the praise.

'She loves to draw!' Elsa confirmed, helping herself to some coffee from the percolator and bringing it to the table to join them.

'Yes,' Miriam agreed, in the midst of opening a cupboard and selecting some cereal boxes. 'But even the greatest artists have to eat before they start their day! Which cereal will you have this morning, my sweet?'

'Good morning, everyone.'

Into all the activity, Nikolai arrived, dressed smartly in a charcoal-grey tailored suit to die for, clean-shaven and showered. His arresting cologne lightly permeated the air.

Gazing at him as an archaeologist might gaze at the find of her life—in wonder, awe and gratitude—Ellie knew her longing for him had no bounds. There had been no conflict in her mind at all last night, when he had told her she could leave. He thought he'd given her a viable option. Ellie knew there *was* no option! She loved him, and she loved Arina, and there was no question of her leaving. All she had to do now was convince Nikolai that she meant it, and pray he wanted her to stay too.

'Ellie? Will you step into my study for a moment?' His glance was fleeting, almost as if he dared not risk looking at her for long, in case he exposed his true feelings.

'Of course…Arina, darling, do you mind if I catch up with you later? If you're gone when I come back, have a great day at school, won't you? I'm looking forward to hearing all about what you've done!'

'Shall I draw you another picture?' Arina asked with excitement in her eyes as Ellie helped her down from the table.

'That would be lovely!'

'You should not tell Arina you will be here when she gets home if you are planning on leaving today!' Nikolai scolded Ellie once they'd reached his study and he had shut the door firmly behind them.

'I never told you I was leaving!'

The tension rolling off his broad shoulders was palpable, and Ellie's heart welled with love and sorrow at the pain he was obviously going through, believing that she was going to walk out on him.

Walking right up to him, and ignoring the look of puzzlement on his handsome sculpted face, she began to straighten the blue silk tie he wore. It didn't need straightening at all, but Ellie could no longer put off being near him or touching him for another second!

'*This* is my home now…here with you and Arina. The only reason I would even contemplate leaving is if you tell me right to my face you don't want me here.'

'Why would you want to stay? I have not made any of this easy for you. I have blamed you and punished you, even *forced* you into agreeing to marry me because of my inability to believe in your innate goodness…to trust you. No one could blame you for hating me under the circumstances!'

'Hate you?' Hot tears swam into Ellie's eyes. 'Oh, Nikolai—I don't hate you! I *love* you! Don't you know that by now? Why do you think I didn't go with any man all these years? It was you and only you I yearned to be with!'

'It was?' He appeared genuinely stunned.

Smiling now, as well as crying, Ellie kissed him gently on the mouth and touched her palm to his smoothly shaved cheek. 'I think I had a crush on you from the very first day I saw you! I told myself it was just a silly fantasy, and that a man like you would never look at a girl like me in that way. But then I saw how tender and loving you were with Arina and it melted my heart, Nikolai! It made me wonder how it would be to have a man who was capable of giving so much love to a motherless child—give some of that love to *me.*'

'I will show you, my darling…I will show you how it will be—because I too have loved you from the first! From the moment I saw how wonderful and natural you were with Arina I yearned to make you my wife…for us to be a real family! But of course I was still married at the time, and then the accident happened. My plans for the future all turned to dust. I *never* would have prosecuted you or your father for the theft of the necklace. I only said that to manipulate you into agreeing to marry me. Do you believe me?'

'I do. You're a good man, Nikolai. The very best! Not many men would take their brother's child, raise her as his own and be so utterly devoted to her! And it must have been devastating for you to lose your only brother in such a tragic way… I've thought about that many times over the years, even though I couldn't recall how it had happened. I could understand you being angry as well as hurt, and wanting to blame someone for what happened.'

'I should have trusted you…seen more clearly the treasure I had in front of me instead of thinking you had betrayed me! It was only because of my lack of faith in love and relationships that I did so, Ellie.'

'But you trust me now?'

'With my life!'

With her heart singing at the idea that Nikolai really and truly loved her, Ellie boldly moved her hands away from his tie, to slide them down the front of his shirt and undo the button on his jacket.

'What are you doing?' Capturing her hand, he deliberately stilled it.

Her heart started to race in case he had changed his mind and did not want her after all. 'I was wondering…'

'Yes?' He was trying to look stern but failing miserably.

Seeing the smile that kept tugging at his delicious mouth, Ellie immediately relaxed.

'I was wondering if you had to dash off to work early today?'

'Why? Is there something you need?'

'Oh, yes!' Ellie started to push his jacket off his shoulders, and this time Nikolai made no move to stop her. 'I need *you*, my love… What I mean to say is,' she started, unknotting his tie, 'I need you right now!'

There was no preamble to their urgent lovemaking. Too impatient to divest Ellie of her skirt and blouse before achieving the erotic union with her body that he craved, Nikolai pulled her to the floor with him. Down to the deep, tightly woven pile of the exquisite hand-made rug he had bartered for with a stallholder in Istanbul many years ago, because it was the custom. He slid her white cotton panties over her bare legs and thrust deep inside her. At the low moan she released he bent to kiss her, and it was as though a fire in him that had been simmering hotly inside his blood for years suddenly burst into an inferno of need and passion. He loved this woman so much! And finally learning that she loved him too had fostered in Nikolai a deep and abiding belief in miracles.

Ellie would be his light and his joy in the years to come—of that he had no doubt. And when Arina had grown and left home—along with any other the children he prayed they might have together—she would continue to be the lover, friend, ally and companion he had always hoped for.

Her heat and delicious melting softness drawing him closer and closer to the edge, Nikolai gazed down into her bewitchingly lovely face, seeing that she too was about to slide deeply into bliss.

'*Ti viy-desh za me-nya*?' he murmured, before ejecting his seed deep inside her.

'What does that mean?' She clung to him, her body trembling in the aftermath of their urgent loving, arms tight round his shoulders.

Breathing hard, and shaking his head in wonder at the unbelievable pleasure that was making every cell in his body vibrate with joy, Nikolai gave a smile that was infinitely tender. 'I just asked you to marry me,' he explained.

'Didn't I already agree to?' she teased.

'I want you to marry me of your own free will, Ellie… Not because I have coerced you!'

'I know that, my love.' She sighed, drawing his face down to hers. 'And I am…I will! It's what I want more than anything in the world… You, me and Arina… A real family at last!'

EPILOGUE

In the garden of his childhood home six weeks later, outside the window of the study that had once been his father's, whoops of joy and laughter rang out, drawing Nikolai away from the article he had been re-reading for a second time—an article in a newspaper his secretary had sent to him from London. The headline read:

PONY-TAILED PSYCHOLOGIST MARRIES RUSSIAN OIL BARON IN FAIRYTALE WEDDING IN MOSCOW

Beneath this was a large black and white photograph of Ellie and Nikolai at their wedding in the cathedral— with Arina as bridesmaid, standing in front of them, carefully holding onto her posy of fresh flowers.

He had heard it said that a man's wedding day was meant to be one of the happiest, most joyous days of his life, and Nikolai could more than attest to the truth of that. The experience had surpassed even his most longed-for dreams. And if they had enjoyed a fairytale wedding, then Ellie had more than resembled a fairytale princess, in the most ravishing of white dresses, designed by one of Italy's top fashion designers. With her flowing blonde hair, sparkling green eyes and the sheer joy that she so naturally emanated, she had been the loveliest bride in the world.

Every day since they had married Nikolai had woken in their bed beside her and counted his blessings. Every day she made him smile, and every day he learned anew just how generous and selfless her heart was. When he had asked her what she would like for a wedding present, after barely a minute's thought she had looked him squarely in the eyes and said, 'A donation for the shelter would be wonderful! Would you mind?'

So the shelter had its donation, and Nikolai's pledged continued support, and he had added even more meaning to this new, happier life he was leading with his interaction and association with the teenagers who for one tragic reason or another no longer had homes of their own.

'Papa! Are you going to come out and play with us? We're playing tag, and we want you to be it and try and catch us!'

Laying down the newspaper on the desk in front of him, Nikolai smiled, got up from the large leather armchair he'd been sitting in, and leaned out of the opened casement window.

'I'm counting to one hundred, and then I'm coming—ready or not!' he exclaimed, chuckling beneath his breath as he left the room and went out to join his lovely wife and pretty daughter…

* * * * *

Turn the page for an exclusive extract from
THE PRINCE'S CAPTIVE WIFE
by
Marion Lennox

Bedded and wedded—by blackmail!

Nine years ago Prince Andreas Karedes left
Australia to inherit his royal duties, but unbe-
knownst to him he left a woman pregnant.

Innocent young Holly tragically lost their baby
and remained on her parents' farm to be near her
tiny son's final resting place, wishing Andreas
would return!

A royal scandal is about to break: a dirt-digging
journalist has discovered Holly's secret, so
Andreas forces his childhood sweetheart to come
and face him! Passion runs high as Andreas issues
an ultimatum: to avoid scandal, Holly must
become his royal bride!

"She was only seventeen?"

"We're talking ten years ago. I was barely out of my teens myself."

"Does that make a difference?" The uncrowned king of Aristo stared across his massive desk at his younger brother, his aquiline face dark with fury. "Have we not had enough scandal?"

"Not of my making." Prince Andreas Christos Karedes, third in line to the Crown of Aristo, stood his ground against his older brother with the disdain he always used in this family of testosterone-driven males. His father and brothers might be acknowledged womanizers, but Andreas made sure his affairs were discreet.

"Until now," Sebastian said. "Not counting your singularly spectacular divorce, which had a massive impact. But this is worse. You will have to sort it before it explodes over all of us."

"How the hell can I sort it?"

"Get rid of her."

"You're not saying…"

"Kill her?" Sebastian smiled up at his younger brother, obviously rejecting the idea—though a tinge of regret in his voice said the option wasn't altogether unattractive.

And Andreas even sympathized. Since their father's death, all three brothers had been dragged through the mire of the media spotlight, and the political unrest was threatening to destroy them. In their thirties, impossibly handsome, wealthy beyond belief, indulged and feted, the brothers were now facing realities they had no idea what to do with.

"Though if I was our father..." Sebastian added, and Andreas shuddered. Who knew what the old king would have done if he'd discovered Holly's secret? Thank God he'd never found out. Not that King Aegeus could have taken the moral high ground. It was, after all, his father's past actions that had gotten them into this mess.

"You'll make a better king than our father ever was," Andreas said softly. "What filthy dealing made him dispose of the royal diamond?"

"That's my concern," Sebastian said. There could be no royal coronation until the diamond was found—they all knew that—but the way the media was baying for blood there might not be a coronation even then. Without the diamond the rules had changed. If any more scandals broke... "This girl..."

"Holly."

"You remember her?"

"Of course I remember her."

"Then she'll be easy to find. We'll buy her off—do whatever it takes, but she mustn't talk to anyone."

"If she wanted to make a scandal she could have done it years ago."

"So it's been simmering in the wings for years. To have it surface now…" Sebastian rose and fixed Andreas with a look that was almost as deadly as the one used by the old king. "It can't happen, brother. We have to make sure she's not in a position to bring us down."

"I'll contact her."

"You'll go nowhere near her until we're sure of her reaction. Not even a phone call, brother. For all we know her phones are already tapped. I'll have her brought here."

"I can arrange…"

"You stay right out of it until she's on our soil. You're heading the corruption inquiry. With Alex on his honeymoon with Maria—of all the times for him to demand to marry, this must surely be the worst—I need you more than ever. If you leave now and this leaks, we can almost guarantee losing the crown."

"So how do you propose to persuade her to come?"

"Oh, I'll persuade her," Sebastian said grimly. "She's only a slip of a girl. She might be your past, but there's no way she's messing with our future."

* * * * *

Be sure to look for
THE PRINCE'S CAPTIVE WIFE
by Marion Lennox,
available September 2009
from Harlequin Presents®!

HARLEQUIN *Presents*

TWO CROWNS, TWO ISLANDS, ONE LEGACY

A royal family, torn apart by pride and its lust for power, reunited by purity and passion

THE ROYAL HOUSE *of* KAREDES

Pick up the next adventures in this passionate series!

THE PRINCE'S CAPTIVE WIFE
by Marion Lennox, September 2009

THE SHEIKH'S FORBIDDEN VIRGIN
by Kate Hewitt, October 2009

THE GREEK BILLIONAIRE'S INNOCENT PRINCESS
by Chantelle Shaw, November 2009

THE FUTURE KING'S LOVE-CHILD
by Melanie Milburne, December 2009

RUTHLESS BOSS, ROYAL MISTRESS
by Natalie Anderson, January 2010

THE DESERT KING'S HOUSEKEEPER BRIDE
by Carol Marinelli, February 2010

HPI 2851

HARLEQUIN *Presents*

International Billionaires

Life is a game of power and pleasure.
And these men play to win!

THE VIRGIN SECRETARY'S
IMPOSSIBLE BOSS
by Carole Mortimer

Billionaire Linus loves a challenge.
During one snowbound Scottish night
the temperature rises with his sensible
personal assistant. With sparks flying,
how can Andi resist?

Book #2854

Available September 2009

EXTRA

TAKEN: AT THE BOSS'S COMMAND

His every demand will *be met!*

Whether he's a British billionaire, an Argentinian polo player, an Italian tycoon or a Greek magnate, these men demand the very best of everything— and everyone....

Working with him is one thing—marrying him is *quite* another. But when the boss chooses his bride, there's no option but to say I do!

Catch all the heart-racing stories, available September 2009:

The Boss's Inexperienced Secretary #69
by HELEN BROOKS

Argentinian Playboy, Unexpected Love-Child #70
by CHANTELLE SHAW

The Tuscan Tycoon's Pregnant Housekeeper #71
by CHRISTINA HOLLIS

Kept by Her Greek Boss #72
by KATHRYN ROSS

www.eHarlequin.com

HPE0909

REQUEST YOUR FREE BOOKS!

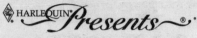 HARLEQUIN *Presents*®

PASSION GUARANTEED SEDUCTION

2 FREE NOVELS PLUS 2 FREE GIFTS!

YES! Please send me 2 FREE Harlequin Presents® novels and my 2 FREE gifts (gifts are worth about $10). After receiving them, if I don't wish to receive any more books, I can return the shipping statement marked "cancel". If I don't cancel, I will receive 6 brand-new novels every month and be billed just $4.05 per book in the U.S. or $4.74 per book in Canada. That's a savings of close to 15% off the cover price! It's quite a bargain! Shipping and handling is just 50¢ per book*. I understand that accepting the 2 free books and gifts places me under no obligation to buy anything. I can always return a shipment and cancel at any time. Even if I never buy another book, the two free books and gifts are mine to keep forever.

106 HDN EYRQ 306 HDN EYR2

Name _____ (PLEASE PRINT) _____

Address _____ Apt. # _____

City _____ State/Prov. _____ Zip/Postal Code _____

Signature (if under 18, a parent or guardian must sign)

Mail to the **Harlequin Reader Service:**
IN U.S.A.: P.O. Box 1867, Buffalo, NY 14240-1867
IN CANADA: P.O. Box 609, Fort Erie, Ontario L2A 5X3
Not valid to current subscribers of Harlequin Presents books.

Are you a current subscriber of Harlequin Presents books and want to receive the larger-print edition? Call 1-800-873-8635 today!

* Terms and prices subject to change without notice. Prices do not include applicable taxes. Sales tax applicable in N.Y. Canadian residents will be charged applicable provincial taxes and GST. Offer not valid in Quebec. This offer is limited to one order per household. All orders subject to approval. Credit or debit balances in a customer's account(s) may be offset by any other outstanding balance owed by or to the customer. Please allow 4 to 6 weeks for delivery. Offer available while quantities last.

Your Privacy: Harlequin Books is committed to protecting your privacy. Our Privacy Policy is available online at www.eHarlequin.com or upon request from the Reader Service. From time to time we make our lists of customers available to reputable third parties who may have a product or service of interest to you. If you would prefer we not share your name and address, please check here. ☐

HP09R